## Brad's gaze

She felt herself ... we met this mo... ...you to call me Brad, you've either avoided calling me anything at all or you've referred to me as Dr Bradley. And if we're not only going to be working together but also living in very close proximity, I think Dr Bradley is going to sound *very* formal!'

'I can see I shall have to try and remember,' said Olivia wryly.

**Laura MacDonald** was born and bred on the Isle of Wight and lives there now with her husband. Her daughter is a nurse and her son is an actor and she has a young grandson. The lovely Isle of Wight scenery has provided the setting for many of Laura's books. When she is not writing for Harlequin Mills & Boon® she writes children's books under the name Carol Barton.

**Recent titles by the same author:**

HOLDING THE BABY

# A SECOND CHANCE
# AT LOVE

BY
## LAURA MACDONALD

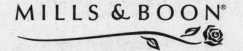

**MILLS & BOON**®

*First published in Great Britain 2000*
*Harlequin Mills & Boon Limited,*
*Eton House, 18-24 Paradise Road, Richmond, Surrey TW9 1SR*

© Laura MacDonald 2000

ISBN 0 263 82247 8

*Set in Times Roman 10½ on 12 pt.*
*03-0007-47794*

*Printed and bound in Spain*
*by Litografia Rosés, S.A., Barcelona*

# CHAPTER ONE

'IT'S not fair—absolutely everyone's going. I'll be the only one who's not allowed—you see.' Hannah flounced out of the room, slamming the door behind her.

Olivia winced then listened as the sound of her daughter's footsteps reverberated through the house as she stomped upstairs, to be followed by the slamming of her bedroom door which seemed to cause the whole house to shake. With a weary sigh she pushed her dark hair back from her face, looping it behind her ear. She really didn't have time for this. A full day loomed ahead of her with two surgeries, a working lunch dealing with paperwork, her house calls and an antenatal clinic. And if all that wasn't enough there was the new locum to interview. The last thing she needed right now was a run-in with her daughter. But she knew this wouldn't just go away. It had to be dealt with.

Taking a deep breath, she crossed the room and, opening the door, stepped out into the hall. At the foot of the stairs she stopped and with one hand on the newel post she looked up to the landing and the circle of closed doors. 'Hannah!' she called.

There was no reply. Olivia felt her irritation rising. She called again, and when she received the same negative response she gave a muttered exclamation, before running up the stairs.

After a sharp rap on her daughter's bedroom door

she turned the handle, only to find, as she had anticipated, that the door was locked. 'Hannah, open this
door,' she said sharply. 'I don't have time for this
now. I'm late as it is and if you don't get a move on
you'll be late for school.'

'I don't care,' shouted Hannah from behind the
locked door. 'I won't go.'

'Oh, yes, you will!' muttered Olivia through gritted
teeth. 'Open this door immediately or not only will
you not go to the party you'll be grounded for the
next week.'

There was further silence from within then there
came the sound of the key being turned, albeit grudg-
ingly, in the lock. Olivia turned the handle again and
pushed, and the door swung open.

Hannah had returned to her bed, after unlocking the
door, and was now lying full length on it. She was
surrounded by a menagerie of cuddly toys while the
walls were so covered by pictures of pop stars there
was barely a square inch of the wallpaper to be seen.
Her dressing-table was littered with make-up, the
chairs and bed were strewn with clothes and the floor
with shoes—everything from platforms to clumpy
boots, from trainers to strappy sandals. Hannah herself, in her school uniform, looked strangely at odds
with the rest of the room.

Olivia had to bite back a remark about the state of
the room, instead limiting herself to drawing another
deep breath and saying, 'Hannah, look, we'll talk further about this tonight but I really don't have the time
now.'

'So what's new?' With a toss of her head Hannah
looked at her mother.

'Hannah, that's not fair,' protested Olivia.

'You never have time. Your work always comes first.' Hannah's face took on a sulky, pouting expression, and as she turned over and sat up Olivia was forced, yet again, to acknowledge how like her father she was with those lustrous dark eyes.

'I try to give you as much time as I can,' said Olivia, holding onto her temper with difficulty. 'But, yes, my work is important, of course it is. It's our livelihood. You know that. Without it you certainly wouldn't have all this.' With a wave of her hand Olivia encompassed the room, the computer, Hannah's music centre and the clarinet on its stand in one corner.

With a sigh Hannah swung her long, Lycra-clad legs to the floor and stood up. At fourteen she was as tall as Olivia and able to look her straight in the eye. 'So you haven't said an actual no, then—about the party?' she said, tossing back her long honey-blonde hair.

'I told you, we'll talk about it again later,' said Olivia. 'I really must go now, Hannah. Mrs Cooper will be in soon. She'll think you've already gone so don't give her a fright when you go downstairs, will you?'

At the door she stopped and with one hand on the handle she looked back at her daughter. 'Isn't your skirt rather short?' she said suspiciously, peering at Hannah's school skirt which barely seemed to cover her bottom and looked decidedly shorter than the regulation length stipulated by her school. 'How many times have you got it turned over at the waist?'

'Only a couple,' muttered Hannah rebelliously.

'A couple?' Olivia raised her eyebrows.

'Well, a few. Anyway, *everyone* does.'

Shaking her head, Olivia left the bedroom. There was no time to get into that particular argument. Miss Fellows, Hannah's form mistress, could sort that one out.

The problem with teenage girls these days, Olivia told herself as minutes later she backed her car out of the garage, was that they grew up too fast. They weren't girls any more. They were young women by the time they were thirteen, or at least they looked like young women with their voluptuous figures, their long legs and their model-type hair and make-up. The problem came over emotional matters when they reverted back to the childhood they hadn't really left behind.

It was a damp October morning, one of those days when it seemed like even the sun found it difficult to get out of bed. There had been severe gales lately, which had stripped many of the trees, and the leaves lay in gardens and along the pavements in great black heaps, clogging the gutters.

Olivia and Hannah lived in a red brick house tucked away in one corner of a little square in the oldest part of the town. The house, built on the site of an old monastery, was called St Ethelred's and was really too big for the two of them, but until a year ago Olivia's mother, Nancy, had lived with them in part of the house which had been converted into a self-contained flat.

If the truth were known, Olivia still hadn't got over her mother's death, and hardly a day went by when she wasn't reminded of her in some small way. Even now as she drove out of the square she thought of her as she caught sight of the huge copper beech, still clinging to its leaves, which Nancy had so loved.

The traffic was always busy at that time of the morning in and around the Wiltshire town of Malsonbury, with people trying to get to work and mothers on the school run, and as Olivia was caught at the third set of lights she sat and fumed impatiently.

At last she reached the health centre—a modern, single-storey building which had been purpose-built for the medical needs of the people of Malsonbury—and pulled onto the car park, noting with a grimace that she was the last to arrive, with the cars of her other two partners parked neatly on either side of hers. The space reserved for the senior partner, James Wilson, was empty as James was absent on sick leave, following a recent heart attack, and the locum who had taken his place had returned to her native Lincolnshire after only two months.

The cars belonging to the practice nurses, the reception staff and to Fiona Clifford, the practice manager, were all parked at their usual places, and as Olivia climbed out of her own car and locked it she knew she was the last to arrive. This was further borne out as she let herself into the staff entrance at the rear of the building and walked through to Reception.

The whole area was teaming with patients, either checking in for the first surgery of the day, waiting to make appointments or collecting repeat prescriptions. Receptionists Lauren and Sarah were working flat out and barely seemed to notice Olivia's arrival let alone the fact that she was much later than usual. Without interrupting anyone, Olivia took herself off to her consulting-room where she met Lucy Scofield, the practice secretary, on her way out.

'Good morning, Dr Chandler,' said Lucy. 'I was just beginning to wonder if you were all right.'

'Yes, I'm fine, thanks, Lucy,' said Olivia, passing the secretary in the doorway and dumping her bag on her desk. 'It was just one of those mornings, that's all. Anything that could delay me, did.'

'I know exactly what you mean.' Lucy pulled a face. 'I've put your mail on your desk, and I've collected your referrals from yesterday. Oh, and don't forget—you're interviewing the new locum this morning.'

'This *morning*?' Olivia had begun leafing through the huge pile of mail on her desk but she looked up sharply. 'I thought he was coming this afternoon.'

'So did we, but apparently he's here already.'

'Well, I can't see him yet—I've got surgery to do!' Olivia retorted. Then, as Lucy would have left the room, with a frown she called her back. 'Does David know he's here?' she said.

'Yes,' Lucy replied. 'Apparently he travelled down last night, put up at the Crown and quite by chance met up with David—er, Dr Skinner,' she corrected herself quickly. 'It seems they knew each other—had met on some conference or other in the past. I gather it was Dr Skinner who told him not to hang around all day but to come in here and get the feel of the place, and the partners would see him as soon as possible.'

'Sounds like David has already made up his mind,' said Olivia with a sniff.

'Maybe he's just relieved,' said Lucy. 'And, you have to admit, we are pretty desperate. Have you seen that crowd out there this morning?'

'Yes, I know.' Olivia sighed. 'But we had no way of knowing the last locum wouldn't stay.'

'I don't think she could stand the pace,' said Lucy.

'Well, let's hope this one will be more suitable. Tell David I'll catch up with him in the staffroom at coffee-time. Then maybe if his friend is still around and Dr Wallis agrees, we could do the interview then. Oh, and, Lucy—ask Lauren to give me a minute and then to send in the first patient, please.'

As Lucy shut the door behind her Olivia slipped off her raincoat, hung it on the hook behind the door then paused for a quick glance in the mirror fixed to the wall. Quickly she ran a comb through her dark hair, and as her father's deep blue eyes stared back at her she lifted the slightly square jaw which was also his. As there came a tap at the door she took a deep breath and prepared once again to enter into the fray.

She worked steadily through the morning, seeing one patient after another, and as she was attending to the last patient on her list her phone rang on the internal line.

'Dr Chandler, there is an emergency just come through for you.'

'Right, Lauren. Who is it?'

'Mr Robinson.'

'Harry Robinson?'

'Yes. He's having a bad angina attack—the warden from his flat is on the other line. Do you want to speak to her?'

'No. She wouldn't call me out for nothing. Tell her I'll come over straight away.'

'Very well, Dr Chandler. That was your last patient on this morning's list.'

Within minutes Olivia was out of the building and in her car again, heading for Harry Robinson's flat.

She found the patient in a great deal of pain from his angina, in a very distressed state and with, she suspected, fluid in his lungs. When he failed to respond to the usual treatment with a Nitrolingual spray Olivia decided to have him admitted to the local hospital.

By the time she'd spoken to the sister in charge of the medical ward and arranged a bed, sent for an ambulance then waited for it to arrive so that she could see Harry Robinson comfortably on his way, it was late morning. When at last she arrived back at the health centre it was to find that both David Skinner's and Scott Wallis's cars were out of the car park, which meant they were already out on their house calls.

Letting herself in at the staff entrance, Olivia decided she would go straight to the staffroom where she would grab a quick cup of coffee, before embarking on her own house calls. Opening the staffroom door, she crossed swiftly to the coffee-machine, which simmered gently for the best part of each day, and poured herself a cupful. Replacing the jug on its hotplate, she picked up the cup and curled her hands around it, drawing comfort from its warmth as she took a sip. It wasn't until she turned and had actually started to cross the room that she realised she wasn't alone. The sight of the man sitting in one of the easy chairs in front of the bookshelves almost caused her to drop the cup.

'Oh,' she said, as her heart thudded against her ribs. 'I didn't see you there... I didn't think there was anyone in here.'

The man continued to sit in the chair as she stared at him, and before he rose slowly to his feet she had noticed that he was large, filling the armchair—not fat, just big. As he stood she saw he was tall, with broad shoulders that filled the tweed jacket he wore. His hair was dark, cut very short, his features regular—the nose slightly aquiline, the jaw clean cut— and the dark eyes had a glitter about them. In fact, thought Olivia as she recovered from the initial shock, too good-looking for his own good.

He held out his hand. 'Dr Chandler, I presume?' An enquiring smile flashed across the handsome features, revealing strong white teeth.

'You presume correctly,' said Olivia, struggling to regain her composure.

'I'm sorry if I startled you. I was asked to wait in here for you.'

'You were?' Olivia frowned for a moment, imagining him to be a medical rep whose appointment she had forgotten.

He nodded. 'Yes,' he replied. 'Duncan Bradley.'

She held out her hand and as it was grasped in a firm handshake she shook her head slightly. 'I'm sorry,' she said, 'but I'm afraid you have the advantage over me...'

'I'm here in connection with the post of locum...?' His accent carried a Scottish burr.

'Oh, yes. Yes, of course.' Her heart sank. Surely not. Not this man. 'I'm sorry. I'd quite forgotten. It's been one of those mornings, you know.'

'Your colleagues said you were rather up to your eyes in things...'

'You've seen them? Are they coming back for the interview?'

'Well, actually, I think they've as good as interviewed me.'

'Really?' Coolly Olivia raised her eyebrows. 'So are you saying it's a forgone conclusion?'

'Not at all,' he replied smoothly. 'Simply that it's down to you now.'

'I see,' Olivia replied slowly. So now, it seemed, she had to contend with the fact that her partners had apparently approved this man in her absence. Slowly she walked to a chair and sat down carefully, setting her coffee on a table beside her.

He followed suit and sat down again opposite her, settling his large frame comfortably into his chair and crossing his legs. He seemed entirely at ease, more so than she did if the truth were known, and again, probably unreasonably, she felt irritated.

'I gather,' she said, 'that you know David Skinner?'

'Yes,' he replied levelly. 'We met at a medical convention a few years ago.'

'Did you know he was a partner here when you applied?' she asked.

'Not at all. It was just one of those coincidences.'

'So why have you applied for locum work?' Suddenly she was curious. Most locums were either very young, wanting to gain experience before they secured a partnership, or at the other end of the scale when they had retired and just wanted a little extra work either to supplement income or to keep mind and body alert. The man before her fitted into neither category, being somewhere, she judged, in his thirties, an age when he should have been at the peak of his career.

'I was with a partnership in Pitlochry,' he explained, 'but personal circumstances forced me to reassess my position. I came to the conclusion that I needed a complete change. I take up a post in a hospital in Canada in a little over four months' time. The time span I would be required to cover here would suit me admirably.'

'You're leaving general practice?' She frowned at the unusualness of the situation and wondered at the personal circumstances that had brought it about.

He nodded. 'Like I say, I needed a change. I saw your advertisement in one of the medical journals and thought it was just what I was looking for to fill the interim months.'

'Have you travelled down from Scotland for this interview?'

He shook his head. 'No, I'm staying with friends in London.'

'And what would you do should we offer you the position?'

'Well, I don't think I'd be inclined to commute.' He grinned and the dark eyes seemed to glitter even more. Olivia found herself imagining the havoc he would cause amongst the reception staff. Before she could comment any further, he said, 'Actually, Scott seemed to think you'd be able to help out over the accommodation problem.'

Olivia felt herself stiffen. 'Oh, I don't know about that,' she began. But that was as far as she got.

'Oh?' he said quickly. 'I understood you have a flat to let.'

'Well yes, but—'

'And that your previous locum stayed there for the short time she was here.'

'That's true but…I, er, I'm not sure I want to let it again…'

'Really?' He raised his eyebrows. 'One of your receptionists came in when the subject was being discussed and she said you had only been saying a few days ago that you would have to find another lodger, and soon by the sound of it.'

Olivia stared at him, for the moment lost for words. She had said that. She couldn't deny it, but the type of lodger she'd had in mind had been more on the lines of the previous one—a respectable young career woman, very quiet and undemanding and entirely in keeping with the house being full of teenage girls— not like the devastatingly handsome male who sat before her. She shuddered as she imagined what Hannah and her friends would make of Duncan Bradley. At last, as he was obviously waiting for her decision, she managed to pull herself together.

'Actually, Mr Bradley—' she began.

'Oh, Brad, please,' he said.

'I'm sorry?'

'Call me Brad. Everyone does…'

'I see. Yes, well. I was about to say that I think we're rather jumping the gun here by talking about accommodation—'

'Oh, I don't know. These things are important.' He gave a shrug.

'Yes, quite. But what I meant was we haven't yet decided on your appointment.'

'Well, I think your partners have so, as I said, I guess it's all down to you…'

'I think I'd rather discuss the matter with my partners first, if you don't mind.' Olivia drained her cup

and stood up. 'Now, if you'll excuse me, Dr…
er…Dr…'

'Brad,' he interrupted.

'Yes, quite…well, I have house calls to make.' She
felt her cheeks suddenly grow warm and hated herself
for it.

He glanced at his watch. 'Perhaps I could come
with you,' he said.

'I hardly think that would be appropriate,' she replied stiffly.

'Why not?' His expression was entirely innocent.

'Well, it hasn't even been decided that you'll be
working here yet.'

'True,' he admitted, 'but I can't see that accompanying you on a few house calls is going to make
any difference one way or the other. It's hardly the
first time I've done house calls so if I don't get the
job nothing is lost, and if I do get the job it can only
be beneficial as it'll help me to get the feel of the
area. Besides, it'll give me something to do to help
pass the time until your partners return and you all
have your confab.'

'Are you expecting a decision today?' Olivia
looked faintly startled. She was beginning to feel very
pressured by this man and she wasn't sure she liked
it.

'David promised I would be told one way or the
other before I go back to London. He said it was only
fair,' he added when he caught sight of her expression, 'especially as I shall have to make arrangements
to go back to Scotland if I'm not wanted here.' He
stood up, towering above her and suddenly making
her feel vulnerable and rather fragile, not something

she was at all used to. 'So, how about these house calls?' he said. 'Shall we go?'

Olivia swallowed. 'Would you mind waiting here a moment?' she said crisply. Ignoring his surprised expression, she put her head down and hurried from the room.

She found the receptionists in a huddle, twittering together, and as she marched up to the desk she had a sudden uneasy insight as to the object of their attention.

'Lauren!' she said sharply, and the youngest of the staff extricated herself from the group and crossed to speak to her.

'Yes, Dr Chandler?' The girl, susceptible to male charms at the best of times, looked flushed and bright-eyed and Olivia's worse fears were confirmed.

'Do you have my house calls for me?'

'Yes, of course.' Lauren turned and picked up a small pile of medical records fastened together with a rubber band. 'Not too many today.' She paused. 'Have you seen him, Dr Chandler?'

'Have I seen who, Lauren?' Olivia was studying the records and didn't look up, but she knew very well to whom the girl was referring.

'The new locum,' said Lauren breathlessly. 'Dr Bradley.'

'I wasn't aware a new locum had been appointed,' Olivia replied coolly.

'Oh.' For a moment Lauren looked bewildered. 'Haven't you seen him yet, Doctor? Dr Skinner told him to wait for you in the staffroom, and when we asked Dr Wallis if he would be appointed, he said there was only you who had to see him and that you would be sure to approve.'

'Really?' said Olivia coolly. As Jill Coburn, the senior receptionist, no doubt sensing trouble, moved forward she added, 'Have you ever had one of those days, Jill, when you feel you must be invisible?'

'Is there anything wrong, Dr Chandler?' asked Jill anxiously.

'No, not really.' Olivia shrugged. 'I was just wondering if it might be a good idea if I were to go back and start today again.' She turned as if to leave Reception then paused and looked back at the girls. 'If my partners return and ask where I am, perhaps you'll tell them that I am on my house calls.'

'Very well, Doctor.'

'Oh, and I suppose you may as well say that Dr Bradley will be with me just in case they are wondering where he has got to.'

# CHAPTER TWO

DUNCAN BRADLEY sat beside Olivia in her small car, looking very cramped in the confined space.

'What do you drive at home?' she asked with a quick but not unsympathetic sideways glance.

'A Range Rover. Not just for my own comfort,' he added, 'but because it's pretty essential for getting to some of the outlying farms and small holdings in the area around Pitlochry.'

'Was that the area where your practice was?' she asked as she drew out of the car park and joined the traffic.

'Yes,' he answered. 'It was a practice founded by my father.'

'Really? And yet now you feel the need to leave?'

'It's time to move on,' he replied. There was a slight edge to his voice and Olivia wondered again what the circumstances were which had made him feel he had to leave a comfortable position in a family-founded rural practice in what was renowned to be a very beautiful part of Scotland. Somehow she had the feeling his reasons involved a woman. She didn't know why she felt that—it was purely instinct.

'My first call is to a new baby,' she said as they drove through the town. 'The mother is very young…'

'How young?'

'Fifteen.'

'That young.' He paused. 'And the father?'

'The boy next door, apparently, and even younger.'

He gave a low whistle.

'Unfortunately, not unusual these days,' Olivia replied.

'Nor in my part of the country.' He paused and looked out of the window. 'I sometimes get the awful feeling that somehow we're failing a whole generation of children.'

'Do you have any solutions?'

'I only wish I had. But I fear the permissive age has moved so far down the line it's impossible to halt it. Maybe it will go full circle one day—who knows? But until it does we will continue to see more and more damaged lives.'

'It is very difficult when a young teenager comes to surgery, seeking contraceptive advice,' said Olivia slowly. 'You know if you refuse, another pregnancy will no doubt be the result...'

'Quite,' he replied, 'but at the same time I get the impression that sometimes these children—because that's what most them are, after all, just children— simply want someone in authority to say no to them. To tell them that what they are contemplating is wrong and that it's far better that they wait until they are older and in a mature and long-term relationship or, even more ideally, until they are married.'

'I don't think you can generalise it like that,' said Olivia. 'Peer pressure is strong. And the media doesn't help—not when it's screamed at them from television programmes and from every magazine they pick up that sex is for fun and implying that provided they practise safe sex nothing else matters.'

They had left the town behind them now and were driving through a heavily populated residential area.

'The house is along here on the right somewhere.' Olivia peered out of the car window, trying to check the house numbers. 'Oh, there it is,' she said a moment later. 'Number eighty-five.'

'What would you like me to do?' he asked as she made to get out of the car.

'You may as well come in with me,' she replied with a shrug.

Without a word he climbed out of the car and joined her on the pavement. Number eighty-five looked neat and well cared for, its net curtains freshly washed and the flower-beds in the garden packed with wallflowers and chrysanthemums.

In response to Olivia's ring on the bell the door was opened by a young girl of around seventeen years of age. She had a baby of about six months in her arms. She smiled when she saw Olivia. 'Hello, Dr Chandler,' she said her gaze flickering to Duncan Bradley, back to Olivia then back to the stranger for a double-take. 'Have you come to see Leanne?'

'Yes, Kylie, we have. Is your mum around?'

'Yes. Come in.' The girl stood back then shouted towards the back of the house. 'Mum! Mum, it's the doctor.'

'And how's Jack?' asked Olivia, touching the baby's hand as she and Duncan Bradley squeezed into the tiny hallway, trying to avoid the baby buggy and the child's car seat on the floor and the mass of coats hanging from a row of hooks on the wall.

'Oh, he's fine, aren't you, Jack?' The girl looked down at the chubby, rosy-cheeked baby in her arms. 'He's teething and he keeps waking in the night but Mum helps with him…'

A door at the back of the hall opened and Olivia

looked up as a woman appeared. Dressed in jeans and a coloured T-shirt, and with her hair screwed back from her face, she didn't at first glance look much older than her daughter, but as she moved into the light closer acquaintance showed that she looked tired, her face drawn and already lined. 'Hello, Dr Chandler,' she said.

'Hello, Tracy,' said Olivia. Seeing the woman's curious look, she added, 'This is Dr Bradley. He's accompanying me on my calls today.'

Tracy nodded. 'I guess you're here to see my new granddaughter,' she said then, not waiting for an answer, she added, 'They're up in the bedroom.' She led the way upstairs and opened the door of a bedroom at the rear of the house.

The new mother was sitting up in bed, surrounded by teddy bears and other cuddly toy animals. Her long fair hair hung limply around her shoulders, and with her white, pointed little face and huge blue eyes she looked no more than about twelve years old. Beside her in a wicker Moses basket lay her baby.

After making the necessary introductions, Olivia asked Leanne how the birth had been.

'All right, I s'ppose.' The girl wrinkled her nose. 'It hurt more than I thought it would. But it was worth it.' Proudly she leaned over to gaze into the Moses basket. 'She's gorgeous.'

'I'll have a look at her in a moment,' said Olivia with a smile. 'It's you I'm concerned with first.' She paused and glanced up at Duncan Bradley, who was peering into the basket. 'Maybe Dr Bradley would like to take baby out.'

'Yes, OK.' Bending down, he drew back the covers and lifted the baby from the basket. His hands looked large and capable against the tiny form in its pink Babygro.

'She didn't take much feed this morning,' said Tracy, and while she and Dr Bradley began discussing the baby's feeding requirements Olivia turned back to Leanne.

'I see from the hospital notes that you have a few stitches,' she said.

'Yes, six,' Leanne replied proudly. 'Kyle only had four when Jack was born.'

'Well, they are the kind that will dissolve,' Olivia went on, 'so have plenty of warm salt baths. Has the midwife been in this morning?'

'Yes,' Leanne nodded. 'She bathed baby for us. I'm dreading doing it. She looked so slippery. I'm sure I'll drop her. I think I'll get Mum to do it for me.'

After further questions concerning Leanne's own eating, sleeping and bodily functions, and while she was entering up her notes, Olivia asked if the baby had a name yet.

'We can't decide,' said Leanne. 'I like Sasha, Mum likes Catherine and Kylie likes Jade.'

'And what about the baby's father? What does he like?'

'I dunno,' said Leanne blankly. 'I don't think he's said.'

'Has he been to see her?'

'Yes.' She nodded. 'He comes in after school.'

'Was he at the hospital when she was born?'

'Oh, no.' Leanne looked faintly horrified, 'He's useless with anything like that. He said he'd probably pass out so I said I'd rather have me mum with me. So she stayed with me all the time, didn't you, Mum?'

Tracy nodded. 'Yes,' she said with a weary smile. 'That's right.'

Olivia turned to the baby. Duncan Bradley had unwrapped her and she was lying on the bed. 'All well here?' she asked.

'Oh, yes.' He nodded. 'She's fine. A good birth weight of seven and a half pounds. Cord is clean and healthy. Feeding is a bit erratic but it's early days yet.'

'They wanted me to breastfeed in the hospital,' said Leanne suddenly. 'But I didn't want to do that. Yuck. It's so messy. At least this way Mum or Kylie can give her a bottle, and later on, when I go back to school, someone else will *have* to do it anyway.'

'Well, it looks like everything is under control,' said Olivia as a little later she returned the baby to her basket. 'I'll call in again later in the week. In the meantime, you'll have the midwife calling each day and the health visitor will also be in. If you do need anything else you know where I am.'

After saying goodbye to Leanne and leaving her with Kylie, who had come into the bedroom with her own baby, Olivia and Duncan Bradley followed Tracy out of the bedroom and down the stairs.

'Thank you, Dr Chandler,' she said as they reached the front door. 'And you, Dr Bradley.'

'That's all right, Tracy,' Olivia replied. 'And you take care of yourself. Don't let them all run you ragged otherwise you'll be ill.'

'Oh, I'm all right,' said Tracy. 'Tough as old boots, that's me. Mind you, I must admit I never thought I'd find myself a grandmother of two and all before my thirty-fourth birthday! It just goes to show none of us know what's round the corner, do we?'

'No,' agreed Olivia faintly. Suddenly she was very aware of Duncan Bradley at her side. 'We don't, and maybe that's just as well sometimes.'

They returned to the car in silence. As Olivia fastened her seat belt Duncan Bradley spoke.

'Tell me,' he said with the air of someone who already knew the answer to his question, 'is there a Mr Tracy?'

'They're divorced,' she replied shortly.

They fell silent again but as they drove back into the town he said, 'You can't think that's an ideal situation.'

'No.' Her reply was sharp, brusque almost. 'Of course I don't. But neither would I want to see a return to old days when a young unmarried girl could be denied any support from her family if she found herself pregnant.'

'You mean the "do not darken my doors again" syndrome?'

'Exactly,' she replied tightly. 'But maybe that's how you think it should be.'

'Of course I don't. But the question of responsibility has to come into it. Take that household, for example. There are what—the two daughters?'

'There's a younger boy as well, from another relationship.'

'Which I guess has also ended?' When Olivia nodded he carried on, 'So you have the mother, the boy and two girls who each have a baby, all living under the same roof in what can be no more than a three bedroomed house. And when it comes to responsibility it's pretty obvious that it all falls squarely on Tracy's shoulders, when in actual fact not only should her daughters be facing up to what they've done but her ex-husband, the fathers of the two babies and the boy's father should also all be playing their parts.'

'I think there have been maintenance agreements— at least from Tracy's ex—' Olivia began, but Duncan Bradley cut her short.

'I'm not talking only about money—although I suspect the brunt of that particular burden is carried by the State—I'm talking about all the day-to-day practical responsibilities of bringing up children. Oh, at the moment it's all wonderful for those girls—to them their babies are little more than dolls and it all seems a game. Just wait until they have a couple of stroppy thirteen-year-olds on their hands and the whole cycle starts all over again.'

'I know what you're saying,' retorted Olivia. 'Of course I do. But I don't happen to think there are any simple answers.'

'Oh, there aren't,' he replied. 'I just think we shouldn't be making things too easy for them, that's all.'

She fell silent and found herself wishing she hadn't allowed him to accompany her on her house calls. She was beginning to feel quite worn out.

'Where to next?' he asked after a while.

She took a deep breath. 'I have to call at the local hospice. I have a couple of patients to see in there.'

Malsonbury's hospice, a large Edwardian house, was set in delightful gardens on the far side of the town. In spring and summer the grounds were a riot of colour, starting with drifts of snowdrops and blankets of crocuses giving way to daffodils, cherry blossom, magnolia and rhododendron and later to masses of roses and great banks of hydrangeas.

Even on a damp, dismal October day the place had

a charm of its own, with tones of russet and copper against deep green conifers lightened by purple-blue clumps of Michaelmas daisies.

'What a charming spot.' Duncan Bradley stood for a moment beside the car, looking around him, and once again Olivia, in spite of herself, was struck by how good-looking he was.

'Yes,' she agreed. 'It is. Are you coming in?'

'Are you going to let me?' He had the grace to look a bit sheepish.

She gave a wry smile. 'No doubt you'll have a few theories as to how the place should be run.'

Matron met them in the hall of the elegant old house. 'Well, hello, there, Dr Chandler. We weren't sure whether to expect you today or not. And who is this?' She turned enquiringly to Olivia's companion.

'This is Dr Bradley,' Olivia replied.

As he shook hands and exchanged greetings with Matron and she heard his accent, she gave a little exclamation of delight. 'Ah, a fellow Scot! Whereabouts are you from?'

'I'm from Pitlochry. And yourself?' he enquired, holding onto her hand a shade longer than was strictly necessary.

'Aberdeen,' she replied, then, glancing at Olivia, she said, 'So, to what do we owe the honour? Have you joined the practice? Ah I know, don't tell me— you're the new locum. Isn't that so?'

'Well…let's just say I'm hoping to be. At the moment it's all down to Dr Chandler whether or not I pass the test.' He grinned at Olivia who, as the matron stared at her, felt decidedly uncomfortable.

'You'll look a long way to find anyone more suited

than a Scot, and that's a fact,' said Matron indignantly.

'There are two ways of looking at it,' Olivia protested mildly. 'Dr Bradley may not like us.'

'I shouldn't think there is too much fear of that.'
There was a gleam in Duncan Bradley's eyes as he
spoke, but there was little doubt that the decision over
whether or not he was to stay in Malsonbury was
firmly down to Olivia.

'Come and see Mrs Hawkins.' Matron bustled
away down the corridor, leaving the two doctors to
follow her.

'How has she been?' asked Olivia as they stopped
outside a door which was wedged partly open.

'Very drowsy,' Matron replied, 'but not, I think, in
any pain. We want it to stay that way so I would like
you to look at the strength of her medication, please,
Doctor.'

'Of course,' Olivia replied as they entered a light,
airy room filled with golden chrysanthemums, where
the radio softly played cheerful music. The patient,
Grace Hawkins, in the final stages of terminal cancer
of the bowel and under heavy sedation, was being
cared for by two nurses.

The usual familiar smells hung in the air—antisep-
tic, medication and bodily odours, masked to some
extent by talcum powder, air fresheners and the fra-
grance of flowers. But underlying all was that sweet,
unmistakable odour which responds to no disguise but
which heralds the end.

Quietly, tenderly, Olivia checked her patient, adjusted her medication to ensure her continued freedom from pain then, after gently resting the back of
her hand against Grace's cheek, indicated she was

ready to go, leaving her patient to the tender care of the nurses.

'Is there anyone else you want to visit today, Dr Chandler?' asked Matron as they walked down the corridor.

'Yes,' Olivia replied after a quick glance at her notes. 'I understand you have a young man here who's a patient of Dr Wilson's.'

'Oh, you mean Stephen. Stephen Trowbridge. He's a day patient. We'll probably find him downstairs in the day room.' Matron glanced at her watch. 'He'll have had his chemotherapy by now.'

'How old is he?' asked Duncan Bradley as they made their way downstairs.

'Seventeen,' Matron replied. 'He has bone cancer but he seems to be responding well to his treatment. He's been leading us a bit of a merry dance, I can tell you.'

'In what way?' asked Olivia.

'Well, we have a man in here, one Samuel Leigh, who fancies himself as an authority on chess. Anyway, young Stephen has been beating him hands down and causing the most alarming ructions in the process.'

Duncan Bradley chuckled. 'Sounds as if he and I might get along.'

'That could be just as well,' replied Matron crisply, 'if you're going to be taking over Dr Wilson's list for a while, with Stephen being his patient.'

Olivia made no comment but she was only too aware of Duncan Bradley's amused expression as they entered the day room.

Like the rest of the house, this was a bright, airy room filled with flowers and plants. A few patients

were occupied with various pastimes, whether reading
the daily papers or magazines, knitting or completing
jigsaw puzzles, but by far the greatest interest seemed
to be centred on the pair seated at a table by the
window, poring over a chessboard. One was an elderly man, his body emaciated by his condition but
his eyes bright and attentive, and the other was a
youth who looked younger than his years. A baseball
cap covered the ravages of chemotherapy, its peak
shadowing the ashen pallor of his skin.

Oblivious to the hush of tension in the room,
Matron bustled across to the table. 'Stephen, the doctors are here to see you.'

Neither man had moved a muscle at her approach
but at her words Stephen looked up. 'Doctors?' he
said in surprise.

'Yes,' Matron replied briskly. 'You have Dr
Chandler come to see you and she has brought
Dr Bradley with her. Dr Bradley will, no doubt, be
Dr Wilson's locum so you may well be seeing more
of him.'

Olivia opened her mouth to correct her, but as
Duncan Bradley moved forward with interest to see
the state of the game and Stephen turned back to the
board she closed it again. What was the point?

It was Samuel Leigh who spoke next. With a scowl
he glared at the newcomers. 'Is this going to take
long?' he barked. 'I intend to beat this young pup
today. He's been getting the better of me lately but
that's only because I've been a bit below par.'

'We won't disturb you for long,' said Olivia. 'I just
want a quick word with Stephen, that's all.'

With a sigh the boy stood up, and with a last lin-
gering look at the chessmen he moved away, follow-

ing Olivia as Matron led the way into her office. Duncan Bradley stayed behind, presumably to chat to Samuel.

'How's it going?' Olivia asked as the door closed behind Matron, leaving her alone with Stephen.

'OK.' He nodded.

'I see from your notes that you were experiencing a lot of sickness after your treatment.'

'I was, but they've changed the tablets now.'

'And these are better?'

'So far, yes.'

'Well, that's good. When do you see the specialist again?'

'In a couple of months. I've got a few more blasts of chemo before then.'

'Do you like coming in to the day unit?'

'Yeah.' He grinned. 'It's all right. I like playing chess with Sam.'

'I understand you keep beating him.'

'That's right.' His face suddenly lit up, affording a glimpse of his former self before the disease had struck. 'Sam's not been well, though,' he went on, growing serious again. 'His last lot of treatment nearly knocked him for six. He was a champ in his day, you know. I was really pleased at first when I beat him.' He paused. 'But I thought I might let him win—perhaps not this game, but in a day or two.'

'That's nice, Stephen.' Olivia smiled and began writing up Stephen's notes.

He was silent for a moment, then he said, 'Are you Hannah's mum? Hannah Chandler?'

She looked up. 'Yes, I am. You know Hannah?'

He nodded. 'Yes, we go to the same youth club. But she likes my mate, Damon.'

'Really?' Olivia said, but silently racked her brain. She knew about Hannah going to the local youth club but she couldn't remember her ever mentioning anyone called Damon—or Stephen, come to that. She felt a sudden swift pang of guilt. Maybe Hannah had been right that morning when she'd said that Olivia was always too busy for her.

'Well, Stephen,' she said at last, after she'd checked that he had no further problems, 'all seems to be going well at the moment. I'll call in again and see you in a week or so...'

'What about that other doctor? Won't he be coming?'

'Maybe,' Olivia replied, 'although at the moment it isn't certain whether he'll actually be taking up the post of locum or not.'

'Can I go back to my chess game now?'

'Yes, Stephen, of course you can.' Olivia stood up and together they returned to the day room where Stephen resumed his game and old Samuel began muttering to himself again.

Five minutes later Olivia and Duncan Bradley took their leave of Matron and left the hospice.

'I'll look forward to seeing you again,' Matron had said to Duncan Bradley as she'd seen them to the door. 'Maybe when I've a little more time we can swap a few stories of home.'

'She seems pretty certain I'll be staying,' he said with a chuckle as he shut the car door and lifted his hand in farewell.

Olivia declined to answer, but when a moment later he asked where their next port of call was her reply was terse. 'Back to the surgery. I have an antenatal clinic this afternoon but before then I need a word with my partners.'

# CHAPTER THREE

'I'M SORRY if you feel we've marginalised you, Olivia, but I honestly thought you would be in complete agreement with us over this.' David Skinner leaned back in his chair and began polishing his glasses.

'I just feel it would have been nice to have been in on any discussions when decisions were obviously being made,' replied Olivia. She and her two partners, David Skinner and Scott Wallis, had met in the staff-room for a late lunch. Sandwiches had been brought in for them and the inevitable coffee-pot was gurgling gently in the corner. She was still feeling very touchy on the subject of appointing a new locum.

'I thought it seemed like a godsend when I met up with Duncan Bradley in the pub then realised he was the one who had applied for the post,' said David. 'It's a long time since I last saw him and I must confess the name didn't ring a bell, but I pride myself on never forgetting a face. Anyway, I really thought he would be ideal. He's the right age and has the right qualifications.'

'What have you got against him, Olivia?' asked Scott between mouthfuls of his ham sandwich.

'I don't know that I actually have *anything* against him,' Olivia replied slowly. 'I just didn't immediately feel he was the one who'd be exactly right for the job.'

'Can you say why?' asked David.

'Not really—just a hunch,' she replied with a shrug. How could she say there was something about Duncan Bradley she found very disconcerting, something about the way he looked at her and about the way she felt far too aware of him when in his company? How could she even suggest to these two men, her professional partners, that intuition had told her that this man was too attractive for his own good and would be sure to cause trouble amongst the staff?

'I don't think we can afford to be too choosy,' said Scott. 'Take the last one, for instance. She quite simply couldn't stand the pace of a busy practice. We certainly wouldn't have that problem with Brad. He's more than capable.'

'If you were concerned about his reasons for leaving his last practice, I don't think you need to worry on that score,' said David. 'He assured me it was entirely for personal reasons. Reading between the lines, it sounded as if he was in a relationship which has ended and, rather than cause any embarrassment, he's decided to move on and eventually make a fresh start in Canada.'

So she'd been right, thought Olivia as she poured herself a cup of coffee. She'd been ready to lay money on the fact that there had been a woman involved.

'There's certainly no one else up for interview,' added Scott. 'And, boy, do we need someone! Last week was horrendous and this week shows no signs of being any better.'

Olivia set her cup down. 'All right! All right!' she said, raising her hands in the air in defeat. 'You win.'

'I'm sure you won't regret it,' replied David soothingly, but there was an air of relief about him as if he had really been fearing a battle, with Olivia digging in her heels as she'd been known to do on occasion when she had felt strongly over some issue.

'Shall I ask him to come in?' said Scott, jumping to his feet. 'He was having a bite of lunch with Fiona, I think.' Not waiting for an answer, he left the staffroom.

'At least now we'll be able to work out some new rotas,' said David, taking his glasses off again and rubbing his eyes.

For a moment Olivia felt sorry for him—he looked so tired. Maybe it was just as well they'd settled this issue. She knew David had been having some domestic problems recently and he could probably well do without any further difficulties at the present time. It had been enough when James had been taken ill, and it was still far from certain what his future role would be within the practice.

It seemed no time at all before Scott was back, this time accompanied by Duncan Bradley.

David replaced his glasses and rose to his feet. 'Come in, Brad, come in,' he said. 'Please, sit down.' He waved his hand towards an empty chair. 'Well,' he went on, coming straight to the point, 'we've had a discussion and we've decided we'd like to offer you the post of locum.'

'That's splendid,' Duncan Bradley replied smoothly. 'I take it you'd like me to start immediately?'

'Oh, absolutely!' said Scott with a huge sigh. 'If we have too many weeks like the last one I think we'll all expire.'

'We'll get Fiona to draw up a contract for you,' said David.

'Great.' Duncan Bradley gave a sigh. 'The only thing I need to sort out now is my accommodation.'

'I thought that was all settled,' said Scott innocently. 'Won't you be renting Olivia's flat?'

'I don't know,' he replied, then turned to look at Olivia who'd felt herself stiffen at mention of her flat. 'I don't think Olivia was too sure she wanted to let it again.'

'Oh, but she does,' said Scott swiftly. 'Don't you, Olivia? Only the other day you said you hoped the new locum, whoever it was, would want to rent the flat, didn't you?'

In the silence that followed, and as three pairs of male eyes turned to her, Olivia knew an answer was required—and not just any answer either, but the one they wanted to hear. The one that would mean the least hassle, the one that would mean the practice could get back to normal and they could all get on with their work and their lives again without all the extra pressure generated by the sudden departure of the last locum.

'Olivia?' prompted David at last as she struggled to answer. 'Are you prepared to let your flat to Brad?'

She took a deep breath and then against every shred of her better judgement she said, 'Yes, I suppose that will be all right.'

'Well, that's wonderful,' Duncan Bradley replied smoothly. 'So I guess all I need to do now is to take myself back to London and collect my gear. And if it's OK with Olivia, I'll come straight back tonight and get myself settled. Then, if I can spend just a couple of days getting used to the place and how things are run, I'll be ready to do my share.'

'Brilliant,' said Scott. 'My girlfriend, Jane, will be

delighted. She says I'm like a bear with a sore head with all this extra work.'

Brad left then, after checking with Olivia where she lived, leaving the rest of them to get on with their work—Olivia, together with the midwife, to take her antenatal clinic and the two men to start their afternoon surgeries.

It was fairly obvious by the end of the afternoon that news of the new locum's appointment had leaked out to the rest of the staff, and as Olivia came out of the treatment room, after seeing the last mum-to-be, she overheard Lauren and Sarah discussing it.

'It'll certainly be nice to have another man about the place,' said Lauren. 'There's a decided lack of available males around here.'

'There's Scott,' Sarah replied.

'Scott's very sweet, certainly, but he's hardly available, not with that sour-faced girlfriend of his in tow. Have you seen the way she looks at us when she comes in here? I'd say she's dead jealous about her precious Scott working with us gorgeous girls day after day.'

'I'd get shot of her if I were Scott. She's the type, after they're married, that'll go through his pockets every night.'

'True. But, like I say, he's hardly available, is he?' said Lauren. 'Then there's David and he's too old...'

'*And* he's married!'

'Oh, yes, there is that, I suppose, even if things aren't too idyllic in that direction at the moment.'

'But, let's face it, we don't know that this one is exactly available, do we?'

'At a guess I'd say he isn't,' remarked Lauren gloomily. 'After all, he is rather gorgeous and gor-

geous men like that are always spoken for. Did you
know he's going to be staying with Dr Chandler?
Lucky Dr Chandler, that's what I say, because
whether he's available or not I guess it would be
pretty interesting, living under the same roof as him.
I tell you, I wish he was going to be staying with
me—'

Olivia decided it was high time she stepped in.
'Lauren.' She spoke a little more sharply than she
might have done as she leaned forward across the
desk, holding out a list. 'Would you find these records
for me, please?'

Lauren turned, her cheeks growing rather pink as
she caught sight of Olivia. 'Oh, yes. Of course, Dr
Chandler,' she said. As she moved forward and took
the list from Olivia she added, 'We were just talking
about Dr Bradley—'

'Yes, Lauren,' said Olivia drily. 'I heard what you
were saying.'

'Do you know if he's married, Dr Chandler?' asked
Sarah, who seemed totally unfazed that they'd been
caught gossiping.

'No, Sarah, I'm afraid I don't know anything about
him,' Olivia replied crisply.

'You have to admit, Doctor,' Sarah went on with
a laugh, 'he is rather dishy, isn't he?'

'Do you think so?' Olivia replied coolly. 'I have to
confess I hadn't really noticed, but now that you come
to mention it, yes, I dare say he would appear attractive to some.'

'But not to you, Doctor? Is that what you're saying?'

'Exactly,' Olivia replied abruptly.

'Oh, well, that narrows down the competition in

our favour.' Sarah laughed again. 'Pity we don't know a bit more about him, though, before we start getting too excited.'

It was true, Olivia thought as she made her way back to her consulting room, they really didn't know anything about him. The personal matter which had been the reason for him leaving his Scottish practice, and which she'd assumed had involved a woman, could just as easily have been a wife as a girlfriend. On the other hand, it could have been someone he'd been having an affair with—the wife of one of his partners, for example. That, no doubt, was just the sort of thing Duncan Bradley would indulge in, she thought grimly. A moment later she felt a swift stab of guilt for having even thought such a thing. After all, the man hadn't really done anything to evoke such uncharitable suppositions.

In spite of that, Olivia really did wish he wasn't going to be working with them and, even more, that he wasn't going to be renting her flat. Already she was kicking herself for having given in over that. After all, it was her flat, for heaven's sake, her home—hers and Hannah's—and she had a perfect right to say whom she did or didn't want there.

Well, she thought angrily as a little later she left the medical centre, all she could do now, having committed herself, was to give it a try and if it didn't work out—if for any reason he caused aggravation—he would just have to go. It was as simple as that.

It was raining, not just the damp drizzle they'd had for most of the day but steady, driving rain that hit the windscreen like steel rods and hammered on the roof of the car. It was barely dusk but the overcast sky made it seem like night and the lights from the shops and the streetlamps threw shimmering reflections across the wet road, making driving conditions difficult.

St Ethelred's, tucked away in its corner of the square, was ablaze with lights which, although welcoming, was at the same time a reminder to Olivia that her lectures to her daughter about conservation were obviously still falling on deaf ears.

She had a slight headache which niggled above one temple but which threatened to escalate into something more serious. Turning off the engine, she sat for a moment, trying to collect her thoughts. It had been such a strange day and it was far from over.

Duncan Bradley would be arriving later so the flat would need to be prepared. And if that weren't enough, Olivia found herself remembering the argument of earlier that day with Hannah and that she'd promised they would discuss the question of the party again later this evening. All this, when what she would really have liked after a full day at work would have been to have poured herself a drink, relaxed in a warm bath, eaten supper then listened to some music or maybe read or watched a film, before going to bed.

With a sigh she got out of the car and put her front door key in the lock. She heard the music even before she opened the door. It throbbed and pounded throughout the house, which seemed to tremble to its very foundations under the onslaught.

For the briefest of moments in the hallway Olivia closed her eyes and rested her head against the door. Taking a deep breath, she opened her eyes, took off her trench coat and hung it up, then purposefully began to climb the stairs.

She met Hannah and her friend Charlotte on the landing. Hannah was obviously saying something but because of the volume of the music Olivia could only see the movement of her lips.

Brushing past the two girls, Olivia entered her daughter's bedroom, crossed the floor and turned the switch on her hi-fi system.

The sudden silence was deafening.

'What did you do that for?' demanded Hannah from the doorway. 'That was Robbie's latest—it's gone straight to number one.'

'I don't care what it was,' said Olivia. 'It was far too loud. I've told you time and again, Hannah, if you continue listening to music at that rate of decibels you'll be deaf before you're thirty.'

'Yes, all right. We know.' Hannah sighed and rolled her eyes. Then she said, 'Are you in now, or are you off out again?'

'No, I'm not "off out again", as you put it.'

'Well, I thought I'd go round to Charlotte's for a while.'

'Actually, Hannah, if you don't mind, I could do with your help,' said Olivia.

'What with?' Hannah looked astonished and Olivia made a mental note to ask her daughter for help a little more often.

'We have someone moving into the flat tonight and I need some help to get it ready.'

'Oh, no! Do I have to?' Hannah rolled her eyes for a second time.

'Yes,' Olivia replied firmly, 'I'm afraid you do.'

'I think I'd better get going,' said Charlotte uneasily.

'So who's this who's moving into the flat?' demanded Hannah.

'It's our new locum at the centre—a Dr Duncan Bradley.'

'A man?' Hannah's eyes widened. 'Well, I suppose that's different, and he's got to be an improvement on the last locum. Old droopy-drawers. Honestly, she was such a drip. Do you know, Charley, she even—'

'That's quite enough, Hannah,' said Olivia sharply.

'Yeah, well…' Hannah sniggered.

'Like I say, I think I'd better be going,' said Charlotte.

'It's pouring with rain,' said Olivia wearily. 'I'd better run you home.'

'No, it's all right, Dr Chandler, really—' Charlotte began but Olivia cut her short.

'Nonsense. I can't let you walk home in this weather and, besides, it's nearly dark. You know the rules.'

Charlotte nodded. The rule amongst all the parents was that none of the girls walked home from anywhere alone after dark.

'I won't be long, Hannah.' Olivia turned and hurried back down the stairs, followed by Charlotte. 'Could you put the oven on?' she called up the stairs to her daughter. 'And when it's heated up, would you pop that lasagne in?'

'Lasagne *again?*' Hannah shouted back.

'Yes, lasagne again.' Olivia grabbed her raincoat and struggled back into it. 'Come on, Charlotte.'

Together Olivia and Charlotte ran for the car. It was still raining, great driving sheets that swept the gardens in the close and the road beyond.

Charlotte's house was about half a mile away, and

as she drove Olivia decided on the spur of the moment to kill two birds with one stone.

'So you're going to this party at the weekend?' she said casually as she drew up at a set of traffic lights.

'Er...no, I don't think so.' Charlotte, taken unawares, threw her a startled glance. 'I don't know,' she added. 'It depends...'

'Depends on what? On how many others are going?'

'Something like that,' mumbled Charlotte.

The lights changed to green and Olivia smiled in the darkness as she let out the clutch.

When they reached Charlotte's house Olivia would have just dropped her off in the drive but the front door opened and her mother stood there. Olivia wound down the window. 'Hello, Frances,' she called. 'All home safe and sound.'

'Thanks, Olivia, that was good of you... But tell me...' Frances Blake leaned forward '...who's on call this evening?'

'It's Scott. Dr Wallis,' she replied. 'Why?'

'Well, it's Thomas, you see. I'm rather worried about him.'

Olivia switched off the engine. 'What's wrong with him?' she asked.

'He's been sick and I think he's running a temperature.'

'Any headache?'

'I don't think so. At least, he hasn't said so... He didn't seem too bad when he first came home from school but he gradually seems to have got worse.'

'I'll come and have a look at him.' Olivia got out of the car and, slamming the door behind her, ran into the house, closely followed by Charlotte.

'This is awfully good of you, especially when you aren't on call,' said Frances Blake.

'Not at all,' Olivia replied. 'After all, Thomas *is* my patient.'

She followed Frances as she led the way upstairs. Thomas, Charlotte's eight-year-old brother, was in his bedroom, lying on the bed. He looked up in surprise as Olivia came into the room.

'Dr Chandler has just brought Charlotte home,' his mother explained. 'She has very kindly said she'll have a look at you.'

'Hello, Thomas.' Olivia sat on the bed, placed one hand on the boy's forehead and with the other she lifted his wrist and located his pulse. He felt hot and feverish and his pulse was rapid. 'Mum tells me you've been sick,' she said after a moment.

He nodded.

'Do you have any headache?'

'No…'

'No stiff neck?'

He shook his head.

'Can I look at your chest and your tummy?'

Obediently he lifted his football T-shirt.

'That looks fine,' Olivia said with a quick glance at Frances, who was hovering uncertainly. 'I'd say he's getting this gastric flu bug that's going around. A lot of children at the primary school are down with it. Make sure he has plenty of fluids, keep him warm and give him paracetamol every four hours.' She looked down at Thomas. 'Looks like you'll be off school for the rest of the week,' she said.

'Will I be able to play football at the weekend?' he asked anxiously.

'We'll see how you are,' Olivia replied. She stood

up and turned to Frances. 'He should be fine now, but if you're at all worried about him during the night ring the emergency number and a night doctor will either give you advice over the phone or come out to him. Goodbye, Thomas.'

'Bye, Dr Chandler,' Thomas replied.

Olivia followed Frances out of the bedroom and down the stairs. 'Thank you, Olivia—I do appreciate that,' Frances said as they paused in the hall.

'That's all right—I know how worrying these things can be.'

'That meningitis scare last month terrified everyone and I'm afraid we tend to assume the worst the minute one of the children shows any symptoms.'

'Thomas hasn't got meningitis,' said Olivia reassuringly. 'But you were right to be concerned. This particular flu bug is not pleasant.' She paused. 'Oh, Frances,' she said, glancing round the hall and satisfying herself that Charlotte was nowhere around, 'about this party the girls want to go to…'

'No way,' said Frances firmly. 'Not an all-night party, not at their age. Geoffrey nearly had a fit when he heard about it.'

'My sentiments exactly,' said Olivia in relief. 'But it helps to know you're not the only one who's laying down the law.'

'Oh, you needn't have any fears about that. I saw a few of the other parents at a meeting last night and they all seemed to be of the same opinion. There will be the usual, inevitable few who will go, of course, but I rather think they will be in the minority.'

It was with a decided feeling of relief that Olivia drove home. It was nice to know she had the backing of other parents when these difficult decisions had to be made.

As she turned into the square she saw that a vehicle was parked at the front entrance to her house in the space in which she usually parked. With a muttered exclamation she drew in behind it and switched off the engine. It was only then, through the driving rain, that she saw it was a dark-coloured Range Rover and it dawned on her to whom it must belong.

She hadn't expected him to get back from London so soon. Obviously Hannah must have let him in. Olivia frowned. Normally Hannah would never have done that—let a stranger into the house when she was alone. On the other hand, she'd known that Olivia was expecting the new locum that evening, she'd known his name and, no doubt, he'd had no trouble in identifying himself.

But, thought Olivia, trust him to turn up before she'd even had a chance to get the flat ready. It was a good job there wasn't too much to do. The flat was well aired from the last occupant, who hadn't long been gone, and Olivia's daily help, Mrs Cooper, ensured that it was kept clean. All that was really required was for the bed to be made up and fresh towels put in the bathroom.

In the normal course of events Olivia would also have put fresh flowers in the sitting-room and stocked up, with milk and bread at least. But there had been no time for any of that and, really, that was Duncan Bradley's own fault for not giving her any time. He could at least have said he'd return the following day, instead of coming back from London that very night. Irritably she climbed out of her car, slammed the door behind her, locked it and ran to the front door through the rain, which at that precise moment was nothing less than a deluge.

She fumbled with her key, and eventually turned it in the lock and pushed the door open. She stood for a moment on the mat, wiping the rain from her face and smoothing back her hair. Then, as she shut the door behind her, she stopped and listened.

Someone was laughing. It was Hannah. But it was the old Hannah, the Hannah Olivia had known before she'd turned into a moody, rebellious teenager. It was the laughter of Hannah, the delightful, sunny-natured child, a sound which recently Olivia had sometimes despaired of ever hearing again.

# CHAPTER FOUR

THEY were sitting at the kitchen table, Hannah with her elbows resting on the table and her chin in her hands as she gazed at Duncan Bradley who sat opposite her. He'd obviously made himself very much at home and was seated well back in his chair, which he had pulled away from the table. He had his legs crossed and his hands behind his head. He'd changed from the formal clothes he'd been wearing earlier in the day for his interview and was now wearing a navy roll-neck sweater and jeans. On the table between them was a tray with two mugs and a teapot.

They were both laughing but they looked up as they became aware of Olivia, standing in the doorway.

'Well, this all looks very cosy,' she said coolly.

'Oh, there you are,' said Hannah as Duncan Bradley lowered his arms and rose to his feet. 'Brad arrived just after you'd gone…'

'Brad?' Olivia raised her eyebrows. 'Don't you mean Dr Bradley?'

'He said I could call him Brad,' protested Hannah. 'Didn't you?' She turned appealingly to Duncan Bradley.

'Absolutely.' He smiled. 'And I'm very glad you are—calling me Brad, I mean. Everyone does. I don't like Duncan, and Dr Bradley is fine on formal occasions or for some of my patients, but with my friends it's different?' Turning slightly, his gaze meeting

49

Olivia's, he said, 'I only hope I can persuade you to do the same.'

Olivia felt herself stiffen at his words. 'What do you mean?' she said sharply.

'Well, since we met this morning and I asked you to call me Brad, you've either avoided calling me anything at all or you've referred to me as Dr Bradley. And if we're not only going to be working together but also living in very close proximity, I think Dr Bradley is going to sound *very* formal.'

'I can see I shall have to try and remember,' said Olivia wryly.

Hannah, who seemed somehow to have picked up on the atmosphere, looked from one to the other with a slightly puzzled expression on her face. 'I made some tea,' she said at last. 'We've had one. Would you like one?' She looked at Olivia.

'Er, no, thanks, not at the moment. I need to sort out the bedding for the flat.' With that she turned and hurried out of the kitchen.

'Damn the man. How dare he?' she muttered to herself as, tearing off her raincoat, she clumped up the stairs. As if he hadn't been irritating enough as it was throughout the day, without swanning into her home when her back was turned and having the gall to charm her daughter into making him a cup of tea— no mean feat, she was forced to admit. In fact, the way things had been recently between herself and Hannah Olivia would even have gone so far as to say pretty well impossible. She could hardly remember the last time Hannah had made *her* a cup of tea, without practically having to be bribed first.

In her bedroom she flung her coat onto the bed then returned to the landing where she opened the door to the airing cupboard and began pulling out sheets, a duvet cover, pillowslips and a stack of towels. She was halfway down the stairs again, the pile of linen and towels in her arms, when she heard a voice from the foot of the stairs.

'Here, let me help you with those…'

'It's all right,' she said quickly, avoiding eye contact with him but only too aware that he stood with one foot on the bottom stair and one hand on the newel post as he gazed up at her. 'I can manage.'

'I don't doubt that,' Brad replied, 'but it doesn't alter the fact that it's because of me that you've been put to all this extra trouble. Come on, let me help— I insist.'

'Hannah was going to help me…'

'She's on the phone—someone called Charlotte, I think.'

'They spend half their lives on the phone,' snapped Olivia in exasperation. This time, however, she made no protest when, on reaching the foot of the stairs, he took the towels from the top of the pile, leaving her with the bedding.

'I'll show you through to the flat,' she muttered, leading the way back past the kitchen through the dining room and into the conservatory, where in the far corner a communicating door opened out onto a small courtyard.

'You have your own entrance here,' she explained as she unlocked a door painted white with wrought-iron hinges and covered in black studs.

'So what you're saying is I won't need to disturb you by traipsing through the house every time I come in or go out?'

It was exactly what she'd meant, although she

doubted whether she would have put it quite that way even given the nature of her mood at that precise moment.

The door opened straight into a small but adequate kitchen with an archway leading to a sitting-room. A further door opened into a bedroom equipped with its own *en suite* bathroom.

'It's rather small,' Olivia began, glancing around, 'and I dare say you'll find the decor too feminine...'

If she'd been hoping that he'd agree and possibly say it was too small and that he'd have to look for something else she was sadly mistaken for, on having a quick but thorough look around himself, he said, 'This is absolutely fine for what I need. After all, it's only for four months—it isn't for ever.'

'No, quite,' she replied drily. Moving rapidly through to the bedroom, she said, 'I'll just make up the bed.'

'I'll help you.' He followed her into the bedroom and when she would have protested, saying she could manage quite well, he spoke again. 'How old is Hannah?'

'She's fourteen.'

'You surprise me. I thought she was older than that.'

'Everyone does. She's at that difficult age,' Olivia added as she took pillows and duvet from the cupboard and began to unfold the sheets and pillowcases. 'Not really a child any more but not an adult either.'

'And your parents?' he asked as he took the edge of the sheet nearest to him and pulled it tight over the mattress.

'My parents?' She looked up and frowned.

'Yes, where are they? Do they live here with you?'

She shook her head, imagining he must have heard something to that effect at the health centre. 'They used to.' She leaned over to tuck her side of the sheet firmly beneath the mattress. 'But my father died ten years ago and my mother…my mother died at the beginning of last year.'

He stopped what he was doing and stared at her. 'I'm awfully sorry—I had no idea.'

'It's all right.' She shrugged. 'How would you have known?'

'And now you and Hannah live here alone?'

'Yes.' She nodded. Picking up the duvet cover, she opened it and began to fit the corners of the duvet inside. 'Here,' she said, 'you take that one.'

Obediently he took the far corner but for the moment his mind appeared to be elsewhere.

'It's very good of you,' he said quietly a moment later.

'What is?' She was concentrating on pushing the duvet into its case and distributing it evenly, and didn't look up.

'Caring for Hannah,' he replied.

She did look up at that. 'Well, of course I'm caring for Hannah!'

'It's not everyone who would take over the care and responsibility of a teenage sister,' he said as he attempted to smooth his side of the duvet.

Olivia stared at him then, slowly straightening up, she said, 'Hannah isn't my sister.'

'No?' He frowned. 'I thought—'

'Hannah is my daughter.'

It was his turn to stare at her, his amazement only too apparent. It was a reaction Olivia had seen before, many times, when people had learned that she had a teenage daughter.

'But she can't be your daughter... You aren't old enough to have a daughter of that age.'

'I can assure you I am,' she replied drily.

'Well...' He seemed speechless for the moment then, spreading his hands apologetically, he said, 'I am sorry. I guess I completely misread the situation. When I arrived here Hannah answered the door. I saw the likeness to you immediately and I asked her if you were at home. She said no, but that you wouldn't be long. I went on to introduce myself and she appeared to know that I would be arriving so she asked me in. We chatted and she made the tea and I have to admit by then I was firmly of the opinion that you were sisters. As I say, never in a million years would I have taken you for mother and daughter—you must have been a child bride!'

Olivia didn't reply, just gave a tight little smile before plumping up the pillows. When she'd finished she glanced round the bedroom. 'I think that's all,' she said, 'so, if you'd like to bring your luggage in, I'll leave you to get settled in.'

'Thank you,' he said. 'Thanks very much, Olivia. I do appreciate you letting me stay here, you know, I really do.'

Suddenly he seemed rather subdued and Olivia felt a little smile tug at her mouth as she made her way back into the house.

She found Hannah still in the kitchen and still chatting on the phone to Charlotte.

As Olivia's gaze met hers Hannah said, 'I'd better go, we haven't eaten yet. I'll see you tomorrow. Yes. Bye.' She replaced the handset. 'He's nice, isn't he?'

she said. Not waiting for a reply, she went on, 'He thought I'd left school.'

'Did he now?' Olivia raised her eyebrows. 'I wonder what gave him that impression.'

'I expect it's because I look older.' Hannah stood up and flicked back the long, honey-blonde hair. 'Everyone says I look older.'

'Well, he isn't under any illusion now.'

'What do you mean?' Hannah demanded, staring at her.

'I told him how old you are.'

'What did you do that for?' retorted Hannah.

'Because he asked,' she replied calmly. 'And because he thought you were my sister—that's why.'

Hannah giggled. 'I think it's really freaky when people think that.'

'Yes, well. I've put him right now.'

'I still think he's nice, and good-looking—even if he is old.'

'He isn't that old,' protested Olivia.

'I told him he could have supper with us.'

'You did what?' She stared at her daughter in exasperation.

'Supper.' The rebellious look Olivia knew so well crept into her daughter's dark eyes. 'There's plenty of lasagne and, let's face it, he wouldn't have anything in to eat, would he?'

'No,' Olivia agreed. 'But I had rather assumed he would choose to eat out.'

'He seemed really pleased when I asked him,' Hannah went on stubbornly.

'Right.' Olivia took a deep breath. 'Well, in that case you can wash a little more salad and cut up some crusty bread.'

Hannah opened her mouth to protest but, catching sight of Olivia's expression, she appeared to think better of it and closed it again.

By the time the pair of them had finished preparing the meal Brad was back, tapping on the kitchen door and pushing it open in response to Hannah's reply.

'I was just wondering,' he said tentatively, 'if your offer of supper still stands?' He spoke to Hannah but his gaze sought Olivia's.

'Of course it does.' It was Hannah who replied.

'Olivia?' he asked.

She took another deep breath. 'Yes,' she said. 'Please, come in and sit down.' She indicated the chair he had occupied earlier.

'This is very kind of you,' he said quietly.

Olivia wanted to say that it wasn't kind at all, that it had all been Hannah's doing. That if she'd had her way she would have had her supper on a tray that night in front of the television but that now she would be forced to sit and make small talk with a stranger when after the day she'd had she was almost too tired to think, let alone to make conversation.

'May I offer a small contribution?'

Olivia had just lifted the lasagne from the oven and as she turned to place it in the centre of the kitchen table she saw that he had placed a bottle of Italian red wine on the table.

'Oh, goody,' said Hannah. 'Wine. I love wine.'

'You can have half a glass,' said Olivia. As Hannah gave a snort of laughter she looked at Brad. 'Thank you,' she said stiffly.

'I'll get the glasses.' Hannah jumped to her feet and, opening a cupboard, took out three, thin-stemmed wineglasses and set them on the table.

'Shall I pour?' asked Brad as Hannah passed him the bottle opener.

'Yes, please,' Olivia replied as she began to serve the lasagne onto the plates.

'You're a Scot, aren't you?' asked Hannah curiously as she watched him pour the deep red liquid into the glasses.

'I am, indeed. I'm from a town called Pitlochry—it's a particularly beautiful part of the country. Have you ever been to Scotland?' He glanced up, looking from one to the other.

'I went to Edinburgh on a school trip once—for the Festival,' said Hannah.

'And you, Olivia?'

'Once,' she said briefly. 'A long time ago. Touring—mainly the west coast, Ardnamurchen, Oban.'

'You must see Pitlochry and the lovely Loch Tummel one day,' Brad said as he sat down. When Olivia was seated he lifted his glass. 'To our new acquaintance,' he said.

Olivia and Hannah raised their glasses in reply and they all sipped their wine in silence, before starting on the lasagne.

'Tell me, Hannah.' Brad set his knife and fork down after a moment. 'What are your plans when you leave school?'

'I'm not sure...' said Hannah.

Olivia set her own fork down and stared at her daughter. 'I thought you'd decided on medical school,' she said.

'Well, yes, I had,' Hannah agreed. 'That was before Jason Summers told me he thought I had what it takes to become a model.'

'And who, may I ask, is Jason Summers?'

'He's the new hairdresser down at that salon in the precinct. He told Charlotte that he used to cut all the top models' hair when he was in London and that I'm every bit as good as any of them. I think I'd much rather do that than become a doctor. It sounds exciting and glamorous, much better than being a boring old doctor, and anyway, let's face it, everyone knows the health service has gone to pot.'

Olivia was having difficulty swallowing her food. Picking up her glass, she took a large mouthful of wine. Brad, who'd been watching her carefully, lifted the bottle again and, without even asking, topped up her glass.

'And have you discussed any of these plans with your teachers?' he asked seriously, before Olivia had a chance to recover.

'Oh, yes,' said Hannah airily. 'I told Miss Booker that after my GCSEs I probably won't bother with A levels.'

'What do you mean, you won't bother with A levels?' Olivia, from somewhere, had found her voice.

'Well, I don't think I'll need them to get into modelling school. I guess brains aren't important, providing you have the looks and the figure...'

'But you have the brains,' spluttered Olivia. 'Do you intend just letting them go to waste?'

Hannah shrugged. 'I can't see any point in going through all that aggro if you don't need to. You said yourself that medical school was tough, it got tougher, if anything, when you were a junior SHO and I wouldn't say you were exactly stress-free now.'

'At least I have a job and probably one for the rest

of my working life, which is more than you can say for modelling,' Olivia retorted.

'That's true,' said Brad. He'd remained silent until that point. 'A model is only in work for as long as her looks last or in some cases until the next pretty girl takes her place.'

'Hopefully before then I'll have made my fortune and be able to retire.' Hannah flicked back her hair in a gesture of defiance.

A hostile silence followed until in an obvious attempt to restore the balance, Brad said, 'So, what hobbies do you have? What do you like to do when you aren't at school?'

'I don't have a lot of time for hobbies,' Hannah replied with a little yawn.

'You used to have a lot of hobbies,' Olivia remarked. Glancing at Brad, she said, 'She used to ride, she attended dancing classes and she was a Guide.'

'Oh, bo*ring*,' Hannah sighed. 'That's all kids' stuff.'

'Well, what about your clarinet? That's hardly kids' stuff but you haven't practised that for weeks.'

'Clarinet?' Brad looked up with sudden interest. 'What's all this?'

'Hannah plays,' Olivia explained. 'Or, at least, she used to. She plays very well and had a place in our local orchestra here in Malsonbury.'

'What do you mean—*had* a place? I still have,' declared Hannah indignantly. 'The orchestra doesn't re-form until the end of this month.'

'And if you don't practise you won't have a place,' said Olivia crisply.

As Hannah sniffed dismissively Brad picked up his

wineglass and began studying its contents. 'This orchestra,' he said at last. 'Can anyone apply?'

'I suppose so,' said Hannah with a shrug.

'And would they take temporary members?'

'They do, don't they, Hannah?' Olivia looked at her daughter. 'They took David's young cousin when he was staying here one year,' she went on to explain for Brad's benefit. 'He played the violin,' she added.

'He was a creep...' Hannah began, then with a frown she turned to Brad. 'Why?' she asked.

'Why what?' He'd finished his meal and, putting his knife and fork together, leaned back in his chair in satisfaction. 'That was really good,' he added to Olivia as she stood up to clear the plates.

'Why did you want to know—about the orchestra?' Hannah persisted.

'Well, I might be interested in joining myself while I'm here in Malsonbury,' he replied casually.

'What do you play?' demanded Hannah eagerly.

'Saxophone,' he said.

'Oh, they'd welcome you with open arms,' said Hannah. 'They lost one of their sax players last year because he moved away and the other is a prat—'

'Hannah!' Olivia turned from the dresser with a bowl of fruit in her hands. 'That's not very nice.'

'Well, he is,' Hannah replied with a shrug. 'I'm only telling the truth. He can't even be bothered to turn up for the rehearsals half the time.'

'Maybe you could take me along with you next time you go and introduce me,' said Brad.

'OK.' Hannah nodded. 'Charlotte goes as well,' she said after a moment. 'She plays the flute.' She stood up. 'Do you mind if I go upstairs?' she asked. 'I don't want any fruit.'

'No, that's all right,' Olivia replied. 'I'm sure Brad will excuse you if you have homework to do.'

'Of course,' Brad began, but he got no further for Hannah cut him short.

'Oh, it isn't homework,' she said. 'I did that ages ago. I have to ring Charlotte.'

'But you were only just talking to her half an hour ago,' protested Olivia.

'I know but I need to tell her something else now.'

'Oh, go on, then.' Olivia helplessly waved her hand, but as Hannah reached the door she paused and looked back.

'By the way,' she said suddenly, 'about the party at the weekend.'

'Yes?' said Olivia, bracing herself for further battle. 'I haven't forgotten. I know I said I'd discuss it with you this evening but maybe you could wait until a bit later...' What she'd meant had been until after Brad had gone. Somehow she didn't think she could face yet more conflict with her daughter in front of this man. He must already be thinking they were permanently at loggerheads.

'No, it's all right,' said Hannah flippantly. 'We don't need to talk about it any more.'

'And why is that?' Olivia stopped, waiting to hear Hannah say again that absolutely everyone was going and that it was really unfair of her mother to expect her to be the only one who couldn't go. At least now, after her conversation with Frances Blake, she had some ammunition.

'Because I've decided not to go anyway,' Hannah declared.

Olivia caught her breath. 'And may I ask what has

brought about this sudden change of heart?' she asked.

'I'm not interested,' said Hannah with a shrug. 'There are only kids going, by the sound of it, so Charlotte and I have decided not to bother.' With that she was gone, out of the kitchen and away up the stairs to her bedroom.

'Hmm,' said Olivia, 'that's not quite the way I heard it.'

'What do you mean?' Brad raised his eyebrows, amusement in his expression.

'Well, when I was talking to Charlotte's mother earlier this evening she gave me to understand that most of the parents had agreed not to let the girls go to this particular party.'

'What is it exactly?'

'An all-night rave, apparently, in some disused barn in the countryside outside Malsonbury.'

'Very wise, too, not letting them go,' agreed Brad.

'I'm just relieved they've changed their mind about going,' said Olivia. 'I honestly thought I was in for another battle just then.' She sighed. 'Hannah didn't use to be this difficult. It doesn't seem that long ago when she was just a delightful little girl, playing with her Barbie dolls and going to ballet and music lessons.'

'I guess it's called growing up,' he said.

'Hmm, yes, well, I hope she isn't serious about this modelling lark.'

'It's probably just a phase.'

'But she's always been so insistent that she wants to be a doctor.'

'Like her mum,' he said softly.

Olivia looked up sharply and her gaze met his. He

didn't look away and she found herself lowering her eyes in confusion. 'Yes,' she agreed, 'even though I've consistently pointed out the pitfalls of this particular profession...'

'It's early days yet,' he said. 'And she's still only fourteen...'

'Yes, but she'll need good grades in her GCSEs in order to continue with her schooling, and here she is, talking about leaving...' Olivia gave a quick, helpless gesture.

'What about her father?' asked Brad.

He spoke casually—a little too casually—and she threw him a sharp glance. 'What *about* her father?' she said.

'Well, won't he speak to her?'

Olivia shook her head. 'Hannah doesn't see her father,' she said.

'Oh, I'm sorry.' He paused and when it became apparent she wasn't going to volunteer any further information he said, 'Are you and he divorced?'

Olivia stared at him for a moment and then, taking a deep breath, she said, 'No, we weren't married, and I, Dr Bradley, have never been married. I am one of those shocking statistics such as we saw this morning.'

He stared at her in bewildered astonishment. 'I'm sorry...?' he murmured at last.

'It's true,' she said, almost flippantly. 'You see, just like Kylie and Leanne, I, too, was an unmarried teenage mother...'

# CHAPTER FIVE

'I OWE you an apology.'

It was the following morning. Olivia was in her consulting room, going through the morning's mail, and Brad had just tapped on her partly open door and stuck his head round.

'Do you?' she replied coolly, her gaze squarely meeting his.

'Can you spare me a minute? May I come in?'

'Of course. I have a few minutes before I start surgery.' She hadn't seen him that morning at the house as she'd left before him, leaving instructions with Mrs Cooper to check that he had everything he needed.

He came right into the room, closing the door behind him. He seemed to fill the room with his presence. This morning he was a little more formally dressed than the previous evening in dark trousers, a light grey jacket and a deep red roll-necked shirt. He sat down in the chair beside hers, the one usually reserved for patients. 'I'm sorry,' he said. 'I had no idea yesterday about your situation.'

'It's OK.' She gave a little shrug. 'How could you have known?'

'No.' He shook his head. 'It isn't OK. There was me burbling on about responsibilities and burdens...'

'Actually,' she said with a little sigh, 'I agree with most of what you said. I just don't happen to think there are any easy answers, that's all.'

As she was speaking Olivia suddenly became intensely aware of his hand resting on his knee. It was a beautifully shaped hand, the hand of a doctor, a healer, the fingers artistically long, the nails broad with large half-moons. But inexplicably there was something about it that disturbed her and quickly, uncomfortably, she looked away.

'Have you always had to cope alone with Hannah?'

He was speaking again and she had to force herself to concentrate on what he was saying, rather than on his presence so close to her.

'Oh, no,' she said. 'My parents were wonderful. I would have never got through or realised my ambitions without them.'

'So they weren't of the "don't darken our doors again" variety?' He smiled as he spoke, his dark eyes glittering.

'Most definitely not,' Olivia replied. 'I had just left school at the time—I'd just completed my A levels and was preparing to go to medical school. I stayed home, had Hannah and then, while my parents cared for her, I continued with my studies. The medical school was in Bath so I was able to spend all my free time at home. When my father died my mother took over the bulk of the burden alone. I hope, after I qualified, I was able to make things easier for her—at least financially when I secured my partnership. But just over a year ago my mother contracted bowel cancer. She died a year later...'

'It's not been easy for you, has it?' he said softly.

Olivia shook her head and to her horror felt tears begin to well up in her eyes. And if that wasn't enough, Brad, seeing her obvious distress, leaned forward and covered her hand, where it lay on the desk, with his own—that well-shaped hand the sight of

which only moments before she'd found so disconcerting. The warmth from it seemed to flow down into
her own, inducing a strange but not uncomfortable
reaction.

For a brief space of time they remained there,
Olivia with her mind a blank, unable to even think
about anything beyond the sense of closeness of the
moment.

The spell was broken when Olivia's intercom
sounded and she was jolted back to the present.
Pulling her hand from beneath his, she leaned forward, suddenly aware that her cheeks had grown
rather warm.

'Yes, Lauren?' she said. Her voice sounded breathless and a bit squeaky, not like her voice at all.

'Oh, Dr Chandler—is Brad with you?'

'Er…yes, Lauren, Dr Bradley is with me,' she replied.

'We wondered where he was. Fiona is looking for
him. Shall I send her down to your room?'

'Yes, all right, Lauren.' Olivia glanced at Brad as
she switched off the intercom. 'The practice manager,
Fiona Clifford, is coming down. Did you meet her
yesterday?'

'Yes, I did.' He nodded. 'I dare say she wants to
know when I'm going to stop loafing around and do
some work.'

'Were you quite comfortable in the flat last night?'
she asked a moment later, suddenly desperate to break
the silence that had grown between them and which
was threatening to reach gigantic proportions.

'Of course,' he said. 'I don't see how anyone could
fail to be comfortable there—it's a charming flat.'

Fiona arrived at that moment, saving Olivia from

having to make any further small talk. She breezed into Olivia's consulting room in her smart pinstriped business suit, her hair braided into its neat plait. 'Good morning, Dr Chandler,' she said. Adopting the lead that seemed to have been taken by the reception staff, she added, 'Good morning, Dr Brad.'

'Good morning, Fiona.' His face relaxed into his most charming smile. 'I gather you were looking for me?'

'Yes, I wanted to discuss work schedules with you and talk about dull but necessary things, like your P45 and tax forms.' She paused. 'You will, of course, be using Dr Wilson's consulting room. I haven't put you down for surgeries today—I thought tomorrow would be soon enough for that. Maybe today you would like to familiarise yourself with everything.'

'Thank you, yes, that sounds fine. I see you use a computer system here.'

'Are you used to that?' asked Olivia.

He grinned. 'You mean have those barbarians north of the border kept up with the rest of the world?'

'No, of course not.' Olivia felt her cheeks redden. 'I didn't mean anything of the sort.'

'It's probably a different system from what you're used to,' said Fiona diplomatically.

'How much patient information do you have on the system?' Brad turned to look at Olivia's computer on her desk as he spoke.

'We have all personal details for each patient plus their medication chart so all prescriptions can be printed. We also have details of things like recent X-rays, smear tests, scans and blood tests.

'What about specialist consultations and details of surgery?'

'Those details are being entered at the moment.' It was Fiona who answered. 'Lucy and myself are working on it but, as you can appreciate, it's a vast project in a practice of this size.'

'So you're still using written notes as a back-up system?'

'I can't visualise ever doing away with written notes completely,' said Olivia.

'Quite,' Fiona agreed. Looking at Brad, she said, 'So where would you like to start this morning?'

'Well, I think it would be a good idea if I were to attend everything that's going on. Maybe I could sit in on some sessions with the nurses in the treatment room, spend a bit of time seeing how you work the admin side of things, sit in on a surgery then go out on a few more house calls. Do you think anyone would have any objections to any of that?'

'No, I can't imagine so.' Fiona shook her head. 'What would you like to do first?'

'Well,' he replied smoothly, 'if Dr Chandler doesn't mind, maybe I could simply stay here while she does her morning surgery. That way I can observe your computer system at the same time.'

'Excellent idea,' said Fiona crisply. 'Don't you agree, Dr Chandler?'

Olivia wanted to say no, it wasn't an excellent idea, that the last thing she wanted was for this man to be present during her surgery. For heaven's sake, wasn't it enough that he was here at the practice and that he was sharing her home without him sitting beside her while she worked, watching every move she made? Instead, she heard herself say, 'Yes, of course.'

'Are you ready to start surgery now?' asked Fiona.

'More or less,' Olivia replied, saying farewell to

her early morning cup of coffee and the brief, peaceful respite she usually enjoyed before the first patient knocked on her door.

'In that case, Dr Brad, I'll see you later about the forms,' said Fiona, 'and I'll go and leave you both to it.' With a smile she left the room, closing the door behind her. Olivia stared at the door without speaking.

'I'll be very quiet,' he said after a long moment of silence.

'What?' She turned her head and frowned at him, wondering what on earth he'd meant.

'You seem pensive, apprehensive almost,' he said, 'and I can only assume it's at the prospect of me sitting at your elbow while you conduct your surgery, so I was saying I'll be very quiet. So quiet and unobtrusive, I promise you'll forget I'm here.'

Chance would be a fine thing, thought Olivia wryly. The sheer size of the man would never allow him to be overlooked. But it wasn't only that. It was more, much more, and had to do with his presence rather than his size. She was too aware of him, whatever he was doing—whether irritating her with his views or maintaining the rapport that they'd surprisingly found between them over some issues.

On the other hand, she was also aware of the way that he made her feel helpless and fragile, not something she was familiar with—at least not in recent times. In fact, it was so unfamiliar as to be positively disconcerting. If she was honest she didn't even want to analyse it because deep down she knew it was due to attraction—attraction on the most basic of levels, that first raw animal attraction between male and female—and that was the last thing she wanted. She had no time to dwell further on the matter, however, as at that moment her first patient of the morning knocked at the door. A woman of about thirty-five came into the room.

'Ah, good morning, Mrs Driver.' Olivia looked up. 'Please, come in and take a seat.' Brad had moved to a chair behind her, leaving the chair alongside her vacant for the patient, but as she sat down, Janet Driver threw an apprehensive glance at the third occupant of the room.

'Mrs Driver, this is Dr Bradley,' explained Olivia. 'He will be joining the practice for a short while as Dr Wilson's locum. Today he's familiarising himself with the way we do things here. Do you have any objection if he sits in on your consultation?'

The woman still looked rather nervous but she shook her head. 'No, that's all right,' she said, as Brad smiled at her and wished her good morning.

'So, what can I do for you?' Olivia pressed the computer keys that called up the patient's medication chart.

'Well, as you know, Doctor, I came off the Pill last year, and since then I've been having really heavy periods. In fact, they've become so bad that I'm having to take time off work.'

'Are you still at the supermarket, Janet?'

She nodded. 'Yes, it wasn't too bad when I was on the checkout because I was sitting down for most of the day, but now I'm a supervisor I'm on my feet all the time. By the end of the day I feel absolutely exhausted.'

Olivia leafed through the notes in Janet Driver's records. 'I see from your notes that we took you off the Pill because of high blood pressure. What contraceptive measures are you taking at the present time?'

'My husband recently had a vasectomy,' Janet replied.

'I see, so that aspect of things isn't a consideration. Let me just check your blood pressure.' As Janet slipped off her jacket and rolled up her sleeve, Olivia set up her sphygmomanometer on the desk, secured the cuff and positioned her stethoscope.

'That's fine,' she said, after carefully noting the reading. 'One hundred and thirty over sixty-five. The next thing we need to do,' she went on as Janet unrolled her sleeve, 'is to find out whether or not these heavy periods have made you anaemic, so I'd like you to attend the nurse's clinic for a blood test. Make an appointment for that in Reception on the way out.'

Janet nodded, and Olivia continued, 'Now, when was your last smear test?'

'I can't remember exactly…' Janet began.

'Don't worry, I have the details here.' Olivia pressed a couple of keys on the computer and the results of all Janet's smear tests were brought to the screen. 'That's fine,' said Olivia. 'No problems there. The next thing I'll do is refer you to a gynaecologist.'

'I suppose that will mean a hysterectomy,' Janet replied gloomily.

'Not necessarily. It may be found that you have fibroids, which can sometimes be dispersed without removal of the womb. Or you may be found to have a condition called endometriosis which, again, can be treated. While you're waiting for your appointment I'll give you a short course of hormone treatment which should help you.' Bringing up Janet's medication chart to the screen, Olivia added the information to the list, before printing out a prescription.

'Thank you, Dr Chandler.' Janet stood up as Olivia

handed her the prescription. 'I'm beginning to feel better already.'

'Well,' said Brad as the door closed behind the patient, 'that's one satisfied customer—maybe that's set the pattern for the rest of the surgery.'

'I wouldn't count on it.' Olivia pulled a face as she pressed the buzzer for the next patient.

One patient followed another, with a fairly predictable range of ailments for normal morning surgery—an elderly man with prostate problems, a woman with a persistent leg ulcer, a child with earache, a man with a damaged hamstring. The list went on but throughout it all, for Olivia the one overriding factor was the presence of the man behind her. Whatever she did she could feel his eyes on her, whatever she said she found herself waiting, holding her breath almost, half expecting him to interrupt or contradict her. He didn't, but somehow his continuing silence only served to make the whole exercise even more nerve-racking than it might have been.

At last it was over and Lauren phoned through to say that Olivia had seen her last patient. With a sigh she leaned back in her chair and flexed the muscles in her neck.

'Do you have a problem there?' asked Brad.

'My neck and shoulder muscles get very taut when I'm sitting for long periods,' Olivia admitted.

'Let's see if I can relieve the tension,' he said. Before she knew what was happening he was on his feet, his hands were on her shoulders and his thumbs were probing gently but firmly at the muscles in her neck.

Her immediate reaction was to protest, to say that what he was doing was unnecessary, that she didn't need it, but as he rapidly found the source of her pain the protest died on her lips.

'Relax,' he murmured, bending his head so that his mouth was alongside her ear. 'You're far too tense. You'll snap if you don't let go.'

It was true. She *was* tense. But how could she tell him that it was his presence at her surgery which had been the main factor? He'd immediately think the reason for that was because she'd been afraid of making a mistake in front of him, may be responsible for a misdiagnosis, when that had nothing whatsoever to do with it. If only it was that simple.

Slowly, gradually, beneath his hands, those hands she'd recognised as healing hands, she began to unwind, to relax. Eventually, as the pain melted away she gave herself up to sheer, exquisite delight.

There was no telling how long they would have remained like that if the door hadn't suddenly opened.

'Oh!' Lucy stopped on the threshold in confusion. 'I'm sorry…'

Under normal circumstances Olivia might have been covered in confusion herself if she hadn't been so far down that road to bliss. As it was, it was left to Brad to reply.

'It's OK, Lucy.' He was totally at ease and spoke casually, unselfconsciously, as if he was used to being interrupted in circumstances such as this every day of the week. 'Dr Chandler was suffering from a bit of stress—I'm just taking care of it for her.' He stopped, to Olivia's acute disappointment, his hands coming to rest for a moment on her shoulders. For a moment she had the craziest of urges to rest her face against one of his hands. She could quite cheerfully have let him continue for hours, but now that it was over it was almost as if she needed to express her gratitude in some way.

'The man's a genius,' she said at last by way of compromise, but with a wry smile.

'I've always maintained that a thorough massage could disperse many of life's troubles,' Brad replied.

'Maybe some of our patients would benefit from that,' said Olivia. Quite suddenly she found she couldn't look him in the eye, embarrassed by the unexpected level of intimacy that only minutes before she had felt towards him.

'Never mind the patients,' said Lucy with a short laugh. 'You could set up a service for stressed health workers. I guarantee you'd be in tremendous demand around here.'

'Was there something you wanted, Lucy? Can I help you with anything?' To cover her embarrassment Olivia's tone was a little sharper than usual.

Lucy looked surprised. 'Only these letters to be signed.' She placed a sheaf of papers on Olivia's desk. 'And to see if you have any referrals to collect.'

'OK, Lucy, thanks.' Olivia nodded. 'There will be some referrals but I haven't done them yet. I'll let you have them as soon as they're ready.'

'So what's next?' Brad asked as Lucy went back to her office.

'Coffee, I'd say.' Olivia stood up. 'Come on, let's go to the staffroom.' She still felt a sense of confusion, and to cover it she briskly led the way out of her consulting room and down the corridor to the staffroom.

Scott was already there, having finished his own surgery, and barely moments after they arrived they were joined by David Skinner.

'How's it going?' asked David when he caught sight of Brad.

'Fine.' Brad nodded. 'I'm gradually getting to know everyone. I've just sat in on Olivia's surgery — she must be sick to death of me by now, what with moving into her flat as well.'

'In that case, why don't you come out with me on house calls this morning?' asked Scott.

Olivia had been about to pour out her coffee but she stopped, the jug poised in the air, waiting to see what Brad's answer would be.

'That's kind of you, thanks. I'm sure Olivia will be relieved.'

'Not at all.' She replied lightly, without turning from the coffee-machine, but she was aware of a sudden stab of something at his decision to go with Scott which she could only put down to disappointment. Which was crazy, really, when she'd been the one who hadn't wanted him around at all in the first place.

'I'm attending the nurse's clinic this afternoon,' Brad went on, 'and then I think I'll spend a bit of time in the office, going over the admin side of things.'

'Will you be ready to start surgeries tomorrow?' David sounded anxious. 'We really do seem to have rather flung you in at the deep end.'

'It's OK.' Brad grinned. 'I'll muddle through just as long as you're all prepared to bear with me for a week or two.'

'Oh, that's no problem, I can assure you,' said Scott. 'We're happy to have some help, believe me. And I'm sure the others will bear me out on that.' He glanced round at the other two, who nodded and murmured their agreement.

Ten minutes later the intercom sounded, and when Scott had answered he passed the phone to Olivia. 'It's Lauren,' he said. 'She says there's someone in Reception to see you.'

Aware once again of Brad's eyes on her Olivia took the receiver. 'Yes, Lauren?' she said. 'Scott says you have someone to see me. Do they have an appointment?'

'Oh, it isn't a patient, Dr Chandler—'

'Is it a medical rep? Because if it is—'

'No, it isn't a rep either. It's a lady called Alison Vincent. She says she's an old friend of yours…'

'Alison! I'll be right out, Lauren.' As Olivia replaced the receiver and jumped to her feet the men all looked at her.

'Who's Alison?' asked Scott.

'Only my oldest and dearest friend, that's all,' replied Olivia happily. 'We went through school together. She lived right here in Malsonbury until she married Paul Vincent and moved to Bath.' With that she swept out of the staffroom and hurried into Reception.

She saw Alison immediately. She was standing near the door, looking out at the rain—not the torrents of the previous day but a steadily falling, persistent, heavy drizzle. She was looking good. Married life and motherhood obviously suited her. Her soft brown hair—cut shorter now than she used to wear it—shone with health, while her figure looked curvier, more rounded than usual. She was wearing well-cut trousers and a long-line tailored jacket in soft jade, and as Olivia called her name she turned and her hazel eyes lit up.

'Hello,' she said. 'Surprise!'

'It certainly is.' Olivia gave her a warm hug. 'It's lovely to see you. But why didn't you let me know you were coming?'

'It's only a quick visit, I'm afraid. Mum's been a bit under the weather lately and I thought I'd pop down to see her.'

'I haven't seen her for a while. Would you like me to call?'

'Would you? I'd be grateful. I'm not sure if it's serious. But you never know, do you?'

'Is Paul with you?' Olivia glanced at the door. 'And Harry?' she added eagerly.

'No, not this time,' Alison replied. 'They're having a couple of boys' days together.'

'So how is my godson?'

'He's absolutely gorgeous and growing fast. Three next month—I can hardly believe it. Where does the time go? How is Hannah?'

'She's very well. Fourteen now, going on twenty-four.'

Alison laughed. 'I'd love to see her. Maybe I could pop over for an hour or so this evening.'

'Oh, yes, do.' Olivia paused and glanced through her notes. 'Listen, I have house calls to do now. Why don't we visit your mum first…?' She trailed off as she realised that Alison wasn't listening to her. Instead she was staring at a point beyond Olivia, her eyes rounded in surprise.

Slowly Olivia turned to see who or what her friend was staring at.

The other doctors had just come out of the staff-room and were walking into Reception. David

Skinner and Scott Wallis were slightly ahead, but it was the man who walked behind them, Duncan Bradley, who quite obviously was the object of Alison's surprise.

# CHAPTER SIX

'I THOUGHT it was Danny,' said Alison, at last breaking the silence that had grown between them. It was a little later and they were in Olivia's car travelling to Alison's mother's house.

'Really?' Apart from a slight raising of her eyebrows, Olivia's attention remained on the road ahead, and her tone, in uttering the single word, was casual with just the necessary degree of surprise.

'He's the image of him,' said Alison bluntly. 'And you know it,' she added.

'Don't know what you mean...' Olivia shrugged.

'Oh, yes, you do. He's big, like Danny, he has the same dark hair and those eyes—Danny's eyes were just like that. You can't tell me you hadn't noticed because I simply won't believe you.'

'Well, yes,' Olivia mumbled. 'I suppose I had noticed a bit of a likeness, but the physical resemblance is where it ends. He isn't a bit like Danny in other ways...'

'Well, I certainly hope not—for your sake!' Alison exclaimed.

'What do you mean?' Olivia sounded indignant now. With an impatient gesture she flicked on the windscreen wipers. 'Will it never stop raining?' she muttered.

'You were besotted with Danny,' said Alison. 'Obsessed, really,' she added as an afterthought.

'And look where it got me,' said Olivia bitterly.

'I was nearly as bad with Mario,' said Alison drily.

'True,' Olivia agreed. 'But at least you had the sense to see it for what it was and not let things get out of hand.'

They were silent for a while, each busy with her own thoughts, as Olivia took the route out of town.

'It was all rather wonderful, though, wasn't it—that summer? I don't think I'll forget it as long as I live,' said Alison a little sheepishly at last.

'And I certainly won't.' Olivia gave a short, hollow laugh. 'No fear of that.' After a pause, with a quick, sidelong look at her friend, she said, 'But, no, I guess you're right—it *was* rather wonderful at the time, before it all went wrong. Exciting, too, I guess…'

'Trouble was, we'd never met anyone quite like them before, had we? I mean, you could hardly compare Danny and Mario to the average sixth-form boys we were used to.' Alison gave a huge sigh.

'It would have probably done us a lot more good if we'd stuck to those sixth-form boys and not let our heads be turned by a couple of tearaways. On the other hand…' Olivia shrugged again '…it taught me the biggest lesson of my life—you can take what you want, enjoy it even, but there's always a price to be paid…'

'I guess you could say the same for me,' said Alison slowly.

By this time they'd reached the small cluster of houses well outside the town where Alison's mother lived, and Olivia had pulled the car into a small lay-by and switched off the engine. She turned her head and looked curiously at her friend. 'What do you mean?' she said.

Alison shrugged. 'Nothing really. Only that there

are some people in your life that have such an impact
and leave such an impression…' She trailed off but
there was no mistaking to what or to whom she was
referring.

'You mean Mario?' Olivia frowned. She'd never
heard Alison refer to Danny's friend again, not since
that fateful summer.

Alison nodded and when she turned her face Olivia
noticed the wistful expression in her hazel eyes.

'But you're happy with Paul, aren't you?'

'Oh, yes,' Alison replied quickly, 'of course I am.
It's just that…well, I guess there'll never be another
Mario, that's all.'

'Probably, if you met him again now you'd wonder
what you ever saw in him in the first place.'

'Yes, probably.' Alison laughed, then hesitantly
she said, 'Have you ever heard anything from
Danny?'

Olivia shook her head. 'No, nothing.'

Alison sighed. 'I guess they had girls in every
town.'

'I'm sure they did.' There was a note of bitterness
in Olivia's voice. 'Did you ever see Mario again?'

Alison shook her head. 'Someone once told me that
he'd gone back to Italy.' She paused. 'Has Hannah
ever wanted to know about her father?'

'Not really. She may want details one day but I'll
worry about that if and when it happens.'

Alison turned to open the car door, then over her
shoulder she flashed Olivia an impish smile. 'I'd say
your worry at the moment is the Danny look-alike
who's come to work with you,' she said.

'I'm not worried about *him*,' replied Olivia.

'Oh, really?' said Alison innocently.

'Yes, really.' Olivia pulled her bag from the rear seat of the car and locked the doors. 'Believe me, he's the least of my worries at the present time, as you'll realise this evening when you see Hannah.'

'It isn't *that* long since I last saw her,' protested Alison as together, through the rain, they hurried towards a blue-painted gate set in a high privet hedge. 'She can't have changed that much.'

'You just wait,' muttered Olivia darkly.

Alison's mother, Stephanie Barber, opened the door of her bungalow in response to the ring at the doorbell. She looked from Alison to Olivia and back to Alison again, an expression of exasperation crossing her features. 'Alison,' she said with a sigh, 'what in the world are you doing, dragging Olivia all the way out here? I keep telling you there's nothing wrong with me.'

'And I say there is,' said Alison firmly. As her mother stood to one side, she and Olivia crowded into the tiny hallway of the bungalow.

'You're just wasting Olivia's time.' Stephanie closed the front door behind them and ushered them into her sitting-room.

'I think, Stephanie, you'd better let me be the judge of that,' said Olivia.

'Can I get you some coffee?'

'That would be lovely,' Olivia replied, 'but maybe Alison could put the kettle on while we have a chat.'

'All right.' Stephanie shrugged as her daughter took herself off to the kitchen. With a little gesture that suggested defeat, she sank down onto the sofa. She was still an attractive woman at sixty-one, with the fair complexion inherited by her daughter and the same soft brown hair as yet barely touched by grey.

'Are you going to tell me about it?' asked Olivia as she opened her case. 'Or do I have to work it all out for myself? I see from your records that you haven't been to see me for over two years. Is that because you've been well during that time or because you were reluctant to tell me anything?'

'A bit of both really, I suppose.' Stephanie hesitated. 'I've been getting rather short of breath lately, and if I've been exerting myself I've had some chest pain. It goes off quite quickly—that's why I didn't want to bother you with it—but when I happened to mention it to Alison on the phone she seemed to think it was something I should have checked out.'

'Quite right, too,' said Olivia briskly. 'Now, tell me, what sort of exertion are we talking about here— everyday activities or something more strenuous?'

'Housework and gardening,' Stephanie admitted, 'and sometimes when I'm shopping if I forget and start rushing about.'

'What about your badminton? I seem to recollect you once telling me you were in the team at the community centre.'

'I had to give that up some time ago. I simply couldn't keep up.'

'I see.' Olivia turned and opened her case. 'I'd like to sound your heart and take your blood pressure while I'm here. Tomorrow I'd like you to come to the centre for a blood test. I'd also like a specimen of your urine, and while you're there, I'll get our practice nurse to carry out an ECG—that's an electrocardiogram,' she added by way of explanation. 'It's to test the efficiency of your heartbeat.'

At that moment Alison came back into the room, carrying a tray with a coffee-pot and cups and saucers. Both women looked up. 'Alison,' said Olivia, 'will you still be here tomorrow?'

Alison nodded. 'Yes, I'd planned to stay a couple of days...' She paused and Olivia saw a flicker of alarm come into her eyes. 'Why? Is there something wrong?'

'I don't know yet,' Olivia replied. 'I need to do tests, some of which need to be carried out down at the health centre. We'll know more then.'

'I'll go with you, Mum,' said Alison quickly, as she set down the tray and began to arrange the cups and saucers.

'You mean to make sure that I go?' said Stephanie with a wry smile.

'Of course not.' Alison sounded indignant. 'I just thought you might like the company, that's all.'

'It's her heart, isn't it?' said Alison. It was a little later and she had walked out of the bungalow with Olivia to her car.

'Probably,' Olivia admitted, 'although I don't want to commit myself until after the tests have been carried out.'

'I thought it was something like that, but she's so stubborn she simply won't listen to me.'

'We can control it, Alison, probably with medication. You mustn't worry.' Olivia climbed into her car, shut the door and wound down the window. 'Come on,' she said. 'Cheer up—it isn't the end of the world. There are thousands of people on heart medication who live quite normal lives.' She paused. 'Are you still coming over this evening?'

'Yes, I'd love to. Thanks. Will Hannah be at home?'

'She should be, yes.' Olivia nodded. 'With a bit of luck Duncan Bradley will be out…' She trailed off, realising her mistake as she saw Alison's expression change.

'What do you mean—Duncan Bradley? What's he got to do with anything?'

'He's…er…he's staying in the flat at the moment…'

Alison stared at her.

'It's only for a short while—just until James gets back—and then he's going to some new job in Canada…'

'So you mean that gorgeous hunk—who just happens to be a Danny Rickman look-alike—is not only working alongside you at the health centre but also happens to be sharing your home?'

'He isn't sharing my home,' protested Olivia sharply. 'All he's doing is renting the flat, which happened to be empty. It was an ideal solution all round…'

'Oh yes, I'm sure it was,' said Alison with a grin.

'Yes,' said Olivia firmly, 'and what you're implying is utterly ridiculous.'

'Really?' Alison raised her eyebrows. 'And how do you know what I was implying?'

'I know, Alison. I just know, that's all.' With that Olivia turned the key in the ignition, let out the clutch and pulled away.

'See you later,' called Alison with a chuckle.

On the way back to the centre Olivia's thoughts were in turmoil. Of course she'd seen the resemblance between Duncan Bradley and Danny Rickman. She'd seen it from that very first moment in the staffroom when he'd taken her unawares because she hadn't realised there had been anyone there. After the initial shock she had dismissed the realisation, partly because she hadn't wanted to acknowledge it and partly because she hadn't wanted to be reminded of Danny Rickman any more than she was each day when she looked into her daughter's eyes.

What she hadn't been able to dismiss quite so easily had been the attraction that had flared between herself and Brad, an attraction she had been at considerable pains to squash before it turned into something unmanageable. It was all to do with the reason she had been brusque and cool with him since his arrival, and although she'd blamed that on her partners, for interviewing him in her absence and practically promising him the job without consulting her, she knew deep down in her heart those were not the reasons at all.

She might have got away with it as well if Alison hadn't turned up and forced her to face up to the truth—that Duncan Bradley was the image of Danny Rickman, Hannah's father, or rather how Danny might look now after fourteen years. No one else would have spotted either the likeness or the significance—only Alison. Alison, who had been through so much with her in those early days and who knew her so well, probably better than anyone else alive.

She didn't see Brad that afternoon. When she returned to the surgery, after completing her house calls, it was with a vague sense of relief that she found he was already in the treatment room with the practice nurse who was taking her baby clinic.

But to her intense annoyance, Olivia found herself looking for him throughout the rest of the afternoon.

When at last she finished her surgery it was to find that he was no longer in the treatment room.

'Dr Bradley gone?' she inquired casually as she returned her notes to Reception for filing.

It was Fiona who answered. 'Yes, I told him to get along. I thought he'd had quite enough for his first day.'

'Is he prepared to take surgeries tomorrow?'

'He said he was,' Fiona replied.

'I think Rachel had a good afternoon with him,' Lauren interrupted. 'She said the young mums in her clinic adored him.'

'Well, they would, wouldn't they?' said Jill with a chuckle. 'Let's face it, he's absolutely gorgeous.'

'You think so?' replied Olivia coolly.

'Oh, yes…' It was Lauren who answered. Lauren who was looking quite dreamy. 'He's scrummy… Don't *you* think so, Dr Chandler?'

'To be honest, I hadn't really noticed…'

'Not your type, eh, Doctor?' asked Jill with a laugh. 'Isn't that what you told Sarah?'

'So what *would* your type be?' Lauren leaned forward eagerly. 'Go on, tell us. What type do you like? Someone like Leonardo di Caprio?'

'He's a child,' protested Olivia.

'Who, then?'

'Oh, I don't know. Someone a bit more mature, I suppose.' Olivia shrugged.

'How about Harrison Ford?' said Jill. 'Or Kevin Costner maybe?'

'Now you're talking…' Olivia laughed dismissively before, with a wave of her hand, she moved towards the door.

As she made her way to the car park she found

herself wondering just what the girls would have thought if they'd known that Duncan Bradley *was* exactly the type of man she was attracted to.

She had one further house call to make, on the way home, to an elderly lady, Constance Perkins, who had recently suffered a stroke. Constance lived with her sister Maud who, although the elder by several years, had cared for her admirably since her return from hospital.

'How are you coping, Maud?' she asked after she'd examined Constance, adjusted her medication and discussed her care plan.

'Very well, thank you,' Maud replied in her precise manner. 'The community nurse comes in each day and between us we do all that needs to be done. The physiotherapist comes in as well to see Constance.'

'You must get very tired by the end of the day.'

'I'm managing perfectly well,' Maud replied crisply. 'My generation were taught to get on with things and not to complain.'

'Yes, Maud, I know, but you're eighty-four yourself and I don't want you making yourself ill.'

'I've told you, I'm perfectly well.'

'Hmm, maybe. I was wondering... I think Constance would benefit from some occupational therapy, but she'd need to go to the day centre at the hospital for that. Would you be able to cope with getting her ready—say on three days a week—if I arrange for the ambulance to pick her up?'

'Of course,' Maud replied briskly.

Olivia eventually left the sisters' cottage, satisfied that she'd come up with something that would benefit them both—Constance, who needed the therapy, and Maud, who needed some time to herself.

It was quite late when Olivia eventually arrived
home. The first thing she noticed on turning into the
square was Brad's Range Rover, parked not in her
space this time but a little to one side under the bedroom window of his flat. Maybe, she thought as wearily she climbed out of her car, that's where he was,
in his flat, and possibly that was where he would re-
main for the rest of the evening. She didn't want to
see him, especially after the observations Alison had
made—it was all too traumatic.

Her hopes were dashed a moment later when, on
letting herself into the house, she heard the sound of
a musical instrument being played in the sitting-room.
She paused and listened, thinking just for a fraction
of a second that it was Hannah practising her clarinet.
But the sound wasn't that of a clarinet, she realised
that almost immediately. This was a different sound,
more resonant somehow. This was the sound of a saxophone, and a saxophone being played rather well.

Something compelled her to stand and listen before
she entered the sitting-room, allowing the evocative
tone of the saxophone to wash over her. As she was
on the point of moving forward another sound joined
that of the first and she realised Hannah had joined
in. Again she stood and listened. It was some while
since she'd heard Hannah play, and although she recognised that her daughter was out of practice it was
nevertheless satisfying to hear the sound of her clarinet again.

Eventually, as the notes of 'Baker Street' died
away, she moved forward into the light. Hannah was
standing before her music stand with her clarinet in
her hands, a frown creasing the smooth skin of her
forehead. Brad was standing in the far corner of the

room with his saxophone still at his lips, his hands on the keys. For a moment her eyes were drawn to his hands as they lovingly held the saxophone, and her thoughts flew, unbidden, to that morning when those same hands had soothed away her tension.

Even as she watched, Brad must have seen a movement in the doorway or sensed that someone was there because he raised his eyes and his gaze met Olivia's.

Neither of them spoke and as Hannah remained unaware of her mother's presence they continued to stare at each other. He *did* look like Danny, especially those eyes—dark and with that distinctive glitter when he smiled. Alison had been quite right. But she herself had also known it—from the very beginning she had known it—but hadn't wanted to acknowledge the fact even to herself.

'Hi,' he said at last.

Hannah looked up at the sound of his voice, then swung round to see who he was talking to. 'Did you hear me?' she demanded when she caught sight of her mother. Not waiting for Olivia's reply, she said, 'I was rubbish.'

'You need to practise, that's all,' said Olivia, moving right into the room.

'Brad is fantastic. I heard him practising in the flat and it made me want to play again so I asked him to come over here with me. There's more room here than in the flat.' Hannah tossed her long hair over her shoulder. 'Did you hear him?' she demanded.

'Yes, I did,' Olivia replied. Turning to Brad, she said simply, 'It was lovely. Would you play some more?'

'OK.' He looked a little embarrassed, as if praise

was the last thing he expected from her—or a request for more. With a shrug, and not bothering with any music, he lifted the saxophone to his lips again. As the haunting notes of 'Careless Whisper' echoed around the room Olivia sank onto the arm of the sofa to listen. Hannah, with a sigh of resignation, sat down on the hearthrug, hugging her knees as she listened.

Olivia allowed herself to be lulled by the music, drawn out of herself away from the world of tension, of patients and their problems, of the demands of teenagers and of running a home, and into a different world—a sensuous world where every note soothed and caressed, lifting her into another dimension. She found herself watching Brad as he stood there, his legs apart, his eyes closed, as he lived every note of his music.

When he'd finished both Olivia and Hannah broke into spontaneous applause. 'That was brilliant,' said Hannah with a sigh. 'Just wait till the others hear you. Old Batey'll want you to do a solo in the Christmas concert—you'll see. You will be here for Christmas?' she added anxiously.

Brad nodded. 'Yes, I don't go to Canada until the end of January.'

'I wish I could play like you,' said Hannah wistfully.

'There's no reason why you shouldn't.' Brad's tone was matter-of-fact. 'You have a real feel for your instrument…and a passion for the music…'

'You think so?' said Hannah eagerly her eyes shining.

'Yes, I do. You've obviously been well taught. The rest now is practice—just as your mum says.'

Hannah pulled a face. 'Yeah, I know,' she muttered. 'Trouble is, I never seem to have the time.'

'You have to make the time,' Brad replied firmly. To quell the rebellion he could obviously foresee coming, he added, 'Come on, let's have another go— together this time. What have you got there?' He leaned forward to look at Hannah's sheet music. 'This'll do,' he said, selecting a sheet. '"Stranger on the Shore." Come on, after three.'

Just as they started to play Olivia caught the sound of the front doorbell, and with a muttered apology hurried to answer it. When she opened the door she found Alison on the doorstep.

'Hello, I hope I'm not too early.' Alison grinned as she stepped into the hall.

'No, of course not...' said Olivia faintly. How could she admit that, with everything that was going on, she had quite forgotten that Alison was coming?

'Hey, who's that playing?' The smile faded from Alison's face as she unbuttoned her raincoat and lifted her head to listen. 'Is it Hannah?' she asked in surprise.

'Well, it's partly Hannah,' Olivia replied, 'but Brad is accompanying her on his saxophone.'

'Really?' said Alison softly, and suddenly Olivia found it impossible to meet her friend's gaze. 'Well, it certainly sounds wonderful. You didn't say he could play.'

'Didn't I?' Olivia tried to sound nonchalant but knew she was failing miserably. 'Come and listen. I'm sure they won't mind.'

'I'd love to,' said Alison. 'Rather a surprise to find Dr Bradley here,' she went on. 'You seemed to think he'd be well out of the way in his flat, didn't you?'

'Stop it, Alison,' muttered Olivia through gritted teeth.

'Stop what?' Alison turned wide, innocent eyes in her direction.

'You know very well what I mean,' replied Olivia darkly. 'And while we're on the subject, don't you dare mention Danny.'

'Wouldn't dream of it,' said Alison.

'I haven't said anything to Hannah about Brad's resemblance to her father and I think it best that she doesn't know.'

'OK,' Alison replied lightly. 'My lips are sealed.'

# CHAPTER SEVEN

THEY waited outside the door until the final notes of 'Stranger on the Shore' drifted out of the sitting-room then Olivia pushed open the door and they went in.

Hannah looked up and when she saw Alison she gave a little shriek, flew across the room and flung her arms around her. 'What are you doing here?' she cried. 'Is Harry with you?'

'No, no. Harry's at home with Paul. I'm only on a quick visit to my mum because she hasn't been well. But I couldn't come to Malsonbury without seeing my favourite god-daughter, could I?'

'You'd better not,' said Hannah darkly.

'I was listening to you play,' said Alison admiringly, glancing at Brad as she spoke. 'It really sounded very good.'

'That was probably Brad,' Hannah replied with a sniff. Narrowing her eyes, she said, 'You don't know Brad, do you?'

She turned to him as she spoke and he stepped forward, his hand outstretched and the ready smile on his face. 'Actually,' he said, 'I believe I did see you earlier.'

'You did?' Alison replied, taking his hand in hers.

'Yes, at the health centre. You were talking to Olivia.'

'You're obviously good at remembering faces,' she replied with a laugh.

'True,' he said, 'but not so good on names.' He

glanced at Olivia as he spoke, as if awaiting an intro-
duction.

'Sorry,' she said. 'Brad, this is Alison Vincent—an
old schoolfriend of mine, and Hannah's godmother.
Alison, this is Duncan Bradley—more commonly
known as Brad—who's a locum at the centre.'

'And who,' Alison continued smoothly, 'just happens to be a first class saxophonist, if what I heard
just now is anything to go by.'

'He is,' said Hannah. She spoke with pride, as if
Brad was somehow her find. 'He's brilliant. He's going to join the orchestra when it starts up again in a
couple of weeks' time.'

'Alison, you will have a bite of supper with us,
won't you?' said Olivia.

'I'd love to, thanks,' Alison replied.

'Come through to the kitchen,' Olivia went on,
'and we'll leave these two to their music.'

'Mum, Brad can stay for supper, can't he?' asked
Hannah as Olivia and Alison reached the door.

'That's not fair, Hannah,' Brad interrupted quickly.

'Why not?' Hannah retorted.

'Well, I was here last night as well.'

'That doesn't matter. He can, can't he, Mum?'
Hannah quite obviously wasn't to be deterred.

'Brad might have something else he wants to do,'
Olivia began as she saw the cosy, girly chat she'd
envisaged with Alison going straight out of the window.

Hannah rounded on Brad. 'You haven't, have
you?' she demanded.

'Er, no. No, I don't think so,' he replied.

'There you are, you see,' Hannah declared trium-
phantly.

Olivia gave a forced smile. 'In that case you must stay,' she said, while Brad looked at Alison and gave a helpless shrug.

'It beats sitting in the flat on your own,' Alison said with a grin.

'You know I'm renting Olivia's flat?' Brad raised his eyebrows.

'Er…yes…I think Olivia did mention it.' With her head down Alison followed Olivia into the kitchen. 'Sorry about that,' she said hastily as Olivia shut the door behind them. 'You obviously don't want him thinking that we've been discussing him.'

'Oh, it's all right. He seems to get his own way whatever happens.' Olivia gave a weary sigh and opened the fridge to survey its contents.

'He really is very nice,' Alison went on. 'At least, on first acquaintance he seems to be.'

'So was Danny,' said Olivia drily.

'You can't really compare the two. You were very young at the time and Danny himself wasn't much older.'

'Old enough to have a string of girls around the country.' There was a note of bitterness in Olivia's voice.

'I know, but I wouldn't have put Brad down as a womaniser.'

'I have no idea whether he is or not,' Olivia replied lightly. 'Neither am I particularly concerned. It makes no difference to me what he gets up to in his private life. Speaking of which, it's probably pretty colourful anyway.'

'What makes you think that?' Alison frowned.

'Well, what would you make of a successful GP

leaving a family-founded practice in a comfortable rural setting to seek a fresh start in a new country?'

'Is that what he's doing?'

'Yes, he's leaving general practice in Scotland to take up a post in a hospital in Toronto.'

'It need not be because of a woman…' said Alison doubtfully.

'True, but I'd bet a month's salary that it is.' Olivia straightened up from the fridge. 'How does the sound of Spanish omelettes grab you?'

'Sounds wonderful to me.'

'And there's Banofee pie for afters.'

'Even better,' said Alison with a satisfied sigh.

Supper proved to be a lively meal, with the four of them sitting around the table in the kitchen. Brad kept them entertained with stories from his previous practice and Alison regaled them with anecdotes of Harry's latest antics and her life with Paul at their cottage just outside Bath.

'Actually,' she said, as the laughter died away after one particularly hilarious story, 'we're having a Hallowe'en party in a couple of weeks' time. Why don't you all come?' She looked around at the others.

'Sounds good,' said Hannah. 'Could Charlotte come?'

'Of course she can—and you, Brad,' Alison added, without looking at Olivia. 'Maybe we could persuade you and Hannah to play for us.'

'It rather depends on who's on call,' said Olivia.

'Go and look at the rota,' urged Hannah eagerly.

'The new one, which will include Brad, hasn't been drawn up yet.'

'When will you know?' persisted Hannah.

'By tomorrow, I should think,' said Olivia faintly. She was beginning to feel like a fly being drawn into a spider's web. The last thing she wanted was to be making plans for social events that included Brad.

'That's good,' said Alison. 'You'll be able to let me know before I go back. If you can come you could stay over with us—that is, if you don't mind mucking in.'

The party broke up shortly after the meal was over with Hannah taking herself upstairs to phone Charlotte.

'I should be going.' Alison looked up at the kitchen clock. 'Mother will wonder where on earth I've got to.'

Brad stood up. 'Can I give you a lift anywhere?' he asked.

'No. Thank you all the same but I've borrowed Mother's car for the evening.'

'I didn't realise she still had her car,' said Olivia.

'She never drives these days,' Alison replied. 'It's practically brand new and it's just sitting there in the garage.'

'I think I'll also get along now.' Brad looked at Olivia. 'Thanks for the supper. It's my turn next. I doubt you'd want to risk my cooking but maybe you and Hannah would let me treat you to a meal somewhere.'

'You don't have to—' Olivia began but he cut her short.

'I know, but I'd like to.' He turned to Alison. 'Goodbye,' he said. 'It was nice to meet you.'

'And you,' she replied with a smile. 'Don't forget Hallowe'en.'

'I won't. Thanks.' He was gone, out of the kitchen

and down the passage to his flat. Olivia and Alison remained silent until the sound of his footsteps died away.

'Well, I think he's absolutely gorgeous,' said Alison at last.

'Maybe,' Olivia replied cautiously.

'Forget he looks like Danny.'

'That's easier said than done!'

'Yes, but I would say well worth the effort.'

'I don't know what you mean,' Olivia protested.

'Yes, you do,' Alison replied bluntly. 'It's blatantly obvious that you fancy him.'

'Alison!'

'Don't look so shocked. You do. Don't you?'

'I…'

'Go on. Admit it. Not just a bit? Not just a teensy bit?' Alison had leaned forward as she spoke and was looking up into Olivia's face.

'Oh, all right!' Olivia gave a helpless little gesture with her hands. 'Yes, I admit he's very attractive, but…'

'No buts. You fancy him,' said Alison with obvious relish. She sat back in her chair with satisfaction.

'I know you've been trying to pair me off with someone for years,' said Olivia with a sigh.

'True,' Alison admitted. 'But you have to agree you're very hard to please. This is the first time for simply ages that I've seen the slightest glimmer of awareness.'

'Oh, I don't know…'

'It is,' Alison insisted. 'Take that lecturer from the university we fixed you up with.'

'He bored me to death…'

'Yes, well, then there was that friend of Paul's—the computer analyst.'

'You mean the one who never changed his socks?'

'How do you know…? Oh, I see. Was it that bad?' Alison asked curiously after a moment.

'Awful,' Olivia admitted.

'But this one is different. You have to agree…'

'Yes, I suppose he is.'

'I know he reminds you of Danny, but that really doesn't mean anything. He probably isn't like Danny at all when you get right down to it. Let's face it, for a start Danny would never have turned out to be a doctor, would he?'

'Not in a million years,' Olivia agreed.

'Well, then. Listen, why don't you just give him half a chance?'

'You're talking like this, but he might not have the slightest interest in me,' Olivia protested.

Alison stared at her. 'Oh, come on,' she spluttered at last. 'It's as plain as a pikestaff that he fancies you something rotten.'

'I think you must be mistaken,' replied Olivia primly.

'You want to have been sitting where I was at supper. I tell you he couldn't take his eyes off you.'

For a moment Olivia was lost for words, but deep inside her there was no denying the little flutter of excitement that Alison's words had produced. At last she stared back at her friend across the table. 'And what if,' she said, 'all that you say just happens to be true? What if something happens between me and…and Brad? What about when he goes to Canada? Where would that leave me? High and dry, that's what, and probably wishing I'd never started anything.'

'If what I saw tonight has its touchpaper lit,' said Alison drily as she stood up, 'then mark my words— either you'll both be going to Canada or Brad won't be going at all.'

Olivia's dreams were troubled that night and for the first time for years she dreamed of Danny. She finally awoke in a sweat and with her heart thumping uncomfortably. She looked at her bedside clock and saw that it was only just after two. Flinging herself onto her back, she gazed up at the ceiling. Sleep would elude her now for some time, she knew, and almost against her will, but because her dreams had been so vivid and so real, her thoughts slipped far back into the past to the events of that incredible summer.

It had been at the very end of their last term at school and with the A-level exams safely behind them she and Alison had felt a glorious sense of freedom and release.

A travelling funfair had been visiting their home town of Malsonbury, pitching its tents, rides and side-shows on the green. The two girls had gone there on the very first night, and for their first ride had chosen the big roundabout with the red-bridled horses that had risen and fallen as it had whirled faster.

As the dark-haired boy who'd manned the round-about took their money he winked at Alison. To the wail of a siren and the sound of Human League the girls had screamed and shrieked in delighted terror. When the ride had ended and they'd dismounted, be-fore staggering down the steps, the boy had waved to them from his seat in the centre of the ride.

'Try the dodgems next,' he'd shouted to Alison. 'Ask for Danny. Say Mario sent you.'

At the time Olivia had thought nothing of it but since then she'd come to realise that had been the way the boys had worked. They'd taken it in turns to choose a girl, and if she'd had a friend with her who'd also looked all right they'd been directed to the other's ride.

'Are you Danny?' Alison said after they ran to a car and the tall, dark-haired boy with the gypsy looks jumped onto the bumper to take their money.

'Sure,' he replied. 'Who sent you?'

'Mario,' replied Alison breathlessly. 'Mario sent us.'

'Did he now?' Danny gave her a quick grin then immediately turned to Olivia and eyed her up and down. 'I guess this calls for a free ride.'

'Gosh, thanks,' said Alison. 'That's good of you.'

'Don't mention it,' Danny replied. Bending low so that his mouth was level with Olivia's ear, he said, 'Just make sure you're at the entrance at eleven-thirty.' He smelt of engine grease, sweat and candy-floss, and Olivia felt a sudden thrill of excitement.

As the sound of Dire Straits screamed across the dodgem floor and Danny leapt from the back of their car Olivia turned her head and was just in time to see him give the thumbs-up sign in the direction of the big roundabout.

'I'm not sure we should wait,' she said doubtfully later as they lingered near the entrance. 'I'm supposed to be in by twelve.'

'Well, you still can be,' Alison argued. 'Oh, go on Livvy, don't be a spoilsport.'

'Oh, all right.' She gave in at last when Alison said

she'd stay on her own if Olivia wouldn't wait with her, but actually she hadn't needed too much persuading. The memory of the moment Danny's mouth had brushed her hair was still crystal clear in her mind and she couldn't wait to speak to him again. There was something different about these fairground boys. They were rough but exciting, very very different from the boys at the local school she and Alison were used to dating.

The fair had begun to close down for the night as the two girls waited in a state of nervous tension at the entrance.

'Maybe they won't come,' said Alison in desperation.

But they did. Of course they did. And from the moment Olivia looked into the glittering dark eyes of Danny Rickman she was lost.

That first night the boys simply walked them home—there was no time for anything else. Even so, Olivia was late and earned a rebuke from her father who was quite strict about that sort of thing.

'What are you doing tomorrow?' Danny said just before she went indoors.

'You mean during the day?' She was quite breathless, heady with unleashed excitement.

'Yeah.' He nodded. 'We don't start work until four in the afternoon.'

'Well, I'm not really doing anything. School has finished. We left last week.'

'Good.' Reaching out his hand, still grimy with engine grease, he ran the back of his fingers down her cheek. 'We'll meet you at ten outside the fair, darlin'.'

'Yes, all right.' Her voice was barely more than a

whisper as she watched him walk away in his tight blue denims and his checked shirt, his hair brushing the turned-up collar of his leather jacket.

Alison was as excited as she was, and the next day both girls were outside the fairground at a little after ten o'clock. 'Best not be right on time,' Alison said, 'otherwise they might think we're too keen.'

But Olivia was keen and so, she suspected, was Alison. When she caught sight of Danny as he sauntered towards them across the green her heart felt as if it had done a somersault.

'Oh,' Alison cried, 'where's Mario?'

But Mario wasn't far behind and he soon came into sight, running and stumbling across the grass in his attempt to catch up with Danny.

There wasn't much to do in Malsonbury and they soon tired of sitting in its only coffee-bar which, with its old-fashioned jukebox, was like a relic from the sixties.

'Isn't there anywhere else to go around here?' Danny demanded on that first day.

'We could go for a walk,' Alison suggested. 'We could go up onto the Chase and through the woods.'

'Sounds interestin',' Danny said with a laugh. As he slipped his arm around Olivia she felt that stirring of excitement again, only this time it was somewhere deep inside.

They walked right up through Malson Chase then into the cool, leafy splendour of the woods that stretched for miles to the west of Malsonbury. Part of the time Danny held her hand and the rest of the time he had his arm around her shoulders while her arm was around his waist. Once when they stopped and turned round Olivia saw that Alison and Mario were similarly entwined, but at some point after that the two couples seemed to part company and when next Olivia looked there was no sign of Alison and Mario.

'Don't worry about them,' Danny said softly when she voiced her concern. 'We're sure to meet up with them again later.'

With that he led her into a small clearing, sat down on the grass and drew her down beside him. She gazed at his profile, his nose which was slightly crooked, his smooth brown skin and the longish dark hair that curled against the collar of his black shirt, and thought that he was the most beautiful human being she had ever seen. When he turned his head to look at her she felt she was drowning in those wonderful eyes of his.

She knew what was coming, but even so she didn't think she would ever, as long as she lived, forget that first kiss.

She had, of course, been kissed before—several times, in fact—but it had never been quite like this. The feel of Danny's mouth on hers, the weight of his body as he shifted so that he covered her, the taste of him as he forced her mouth to open beneath his—an unfamiliar mixture of cigarettes and peppermint chewing gum—and the sudden thrill that shot through her body when his hands found her breasts through the thin fabric of the cotton blouse she was wearing.

That first day set the pattern for the rest of the fairground's two weeks' stay in Malsonbury. Each morning the girls met Danny and Mario. Sometimes they went to the coffee-bar first, but as the days slipped by at an alarming rate more often than not they found themselves making straight for the Chase and the woods beyond.

It was a truly glorious, carefree time of love and laughter, and for Olivia at least a time of awakening. The weather was warm and sultry and it was a relief to escape from the brick and tarmac of the town to the fresh green of the woods where she and Danny lay for hours in each other's arms.

Every evening the girls visited the fair, occasionally going on other rides or trying their luck on the various sideshows but most of the time spending their money on the dodgems and the roundabout. When their money had been spent they sat on the grass bank, eating hot dogs or toffee-apples, and listened to the music that drifted across the green, waiting for the boys to finish work for the night and walk them home.

To this very day if Olivia heard even a snatch of music from that era she was instantly transported back, so much so that she could smell the candyfloss, hear the sirens wailing on the dodgems and feel the heat from the generators.

More often than not Olivia had been late and in trouble with her parents, but she'd been past caring and as the days had passed a sort of desperation had set in as her parting with Danny had grown closer.

For the first time in her life she'd been in love, but it had been a love that had had a searing, painful edge to it, as if she'd known deep in her heart that it could never have lasted.

'I'll come back and see you,' Danny said when she dared to voice her fears.

'But I won't be here. I shall be going to medical school in the autumn.'

'Then I'll come and see you there, wherever that is—or maybe you could come and see me, wherever we are.'

But somehow he sounded too casual, as if it didn't matter too much to him, and she felt despair.

'Have you—you know—done anything?' Alison asked Olivia. It was one morning towards the end of the second week and they were walking to the green to meet the boys.

'No.' She shook her head. When Alison remained silent, she said quickly, 'Have you?' Alison nodded and Olivia felt a swift stab of envy. 'I think we might, though,' she added quickly, not wanting to appear unworldly in the eyes of her friend. 'Danny wants to…'

'And you? Do you want to?'

'Oh, yes. I love him, Alison. I've never felt this way before.'

'You're not on the Pill, are you?' Alison sounded concerned.

Olivia shook her head again. 'No,' she replied. 'I'd never intended doing anything before.'

'Until you met Danny, you mean?'

'That's right.'

'Olivia?'

'Yes?'

'Be careful, won't you?'

'Of course,' she replied indignantly.

She wanted to. Of course she did. She'd never wanted anyone so much before, but until now she'd somehow resisted Danny. Alison and Mario had done it, but Olivia had known they would because Alison was on the Pill. She had considered going on the Pill when she was dating her previous boyfriend, but deep down she'd known that she hadn't really loved him and after a long talk with her mother she'd decided against the Pill. Now, however, everything had changed. She did love Danny, she knew that without any doubt. There was no time to get advice about the Pill, though, at least not before Danny moved on. So maybe, maybe if they were very careful…

'I love you, Livvy, darlin',' he said. 'Just trust me. Everythin' will be all right.'

Olivia shifted slightly. The first soft fingers of dawn were touching the sky and there was a light patch on the ceiling just above the wardrobe. The hands on the clock now stood at six-thirty and she knew she must have slept again. With a sigh she sat up and swung her legs to the floor. She felt quite wretched, almost as if she hadn't slept. Why, oh, why had she dreamed about Danny again after all this time?

She knew the answer to that without probing too deeply. It was all to do with Brad, who reminded her so much of Danny Rickman that all the memories of that brief but bitter-sweet episode in her life had been churned up to a point where she relived them, not only while she was awake but also whilst she slept.

Somehow she had to try and put all that out of her mind. Brad was here to stay, at least for the immediate future, and somehow she had to live and work alongside him as if his arrival in Malsonbury had had no effect on her whatsoever.

# CHAPTER EIGHT

IF OLIVIA had thought her life might have gone on in the same way after Brad's arrival she was greatly mistaken because, even though during that first week they settled into some sort of routine, nothing was the same as it had been before. At the surgery everyone seemed aware of his presence all the time—he was like a breath of fresh air about the place. At home it was more of the same as he seemed to be directly responsible for filling her house with music and laughter.

There were times, however, she had to admit, when he thought he wasn't being observed, that she caught him in a pensive mood and then, in his eyes, she saw a shadow of something that could only be interpreted as sadness. It was gone almost immediately, leaving Olivia wondering if perhaps she might have imagined it.

When Alison had said it was obvious that Brad fancied her, Olivia had been more than inclined to dismiss the notion, but as the days slipped pleasantly by she began to fall under his spell and to believe it might be true. But, still, he reminded her of Danny and mainly for that reason she held her own emotions in check, not wishing to fall victim for a second time, only too mindful that Brad had his own problems. Aside from that, she was also well aware that he was only passing through, that soon he would go out of their lives for ever.

At the end of Brad's first week Olivia received test results on Stephanie Barber that, as she'd suspected, confirmed heart disease. After giving Stephanie the results, she arranged an appointment for her with a heart specialist.

'Will it mean surgery?' Stephanie looked apprehensive but at the same time resigned.

'Not necessarily. We may find that he'll want to control your condition with medication,' Olivia replied. 'But let's wait and see. Now, you will tell Alison, won't you?'

'Yes, of course.' Stephanie pulled a face. 'I'll be in trouble if I don't.' She paused. 'I understand you and Hannah are going down for Hallowe'en?'

'That's right.' Olivia smiled.

'And your new locum? He's going as well, or so Alison tells me.'

'Yes.' Olivia nodded and wondered what else Alison had told her mother about the new locum.

As Stephanie Barber left her consulting room Olivia's intercom sounded. She flicked the switch and Jill's voice came through. 'Dr Chandler, Matron from the hospice is on line one for you.'

'Thanks, Jill.' Olivia picked up her phone. 'Good morning, Matron,' she said.

'Good morning, Dr Chandler. Just to inform you that Grace Hawkins died a few moments ago.'

'Poor Grace—I'll be over shortly to certify.'

'Thank you, Doctor. It was all very peaceful at the end. Oh, one other thing. Stephen Trowbridge isn't very bright this morning—will you look at him when you come in?'

'Well, as Stephen is really Dr Wilson's patient I'd

better mention it to Dr Bradley,' Olivia replied. 'He may wish to come in himself.'

'Ah,' said Matron knowingly. 'I'm glad to see you took my advice and took that young man on.'

Her surgery over for that morning, Olivia made her way down the corridor to James Wilson's consulting room. She listened for a moment and, hearing no sound of voices within, knocked gently. When Brad's voice bade her enter she turned the handle and pushed open the door. He was seated at the desk behind a mountain of paperwork.

'You look harassed,' she said as he looked up, and she closed the door behind her.

With a sigh he pushed the pile of papers away and leaned back in his chair. 'I understood the age of computers was meant to reduce the amount of paperwork,' he said, 'but in my experience it just seems to have increased it.'

'I agree.' Olivia laughed. 'I very often feel in danger of disappearing beneath it all, never to be seen again.' She paused. 'Apart from that, how's it going?'

'All right, I think.' He nodded. 'It's very strange, taking over someone's list, even if it's only for a short time. Some patients are very suspicious of anyone new while others seem to positively relish the prospect of a fresh ear listening to their worries.'

'There are those who really thrive on second opinions,' Olivia replied knowingly. 'What I actually came to tell you was that Matron at the hospice has just phoned to tell me that my patient there, Grace Hawkins, died this morning. I said I would go over to certify and she mentioned that young Stephen Trowbridge wasn't too well today. Would you like

me to take a look at him for you or do you want to
go yourself?'

'I think I'll go and see him,' Brad replied. 'It's
good of you to offer but he is James's patient after
all. Besides, I need a reason to get away from this
paperwork.' He paused. 'Shall we go together?'

'May as well.' Olivia shrugged. 'I'll meet you in
Reception in—what—fifteen minutes?'

'That's fine with me.' He nodded, his eyes briefly
meeting hers.

Hurriedly she left the room. She still found it disconcerting when he looked at her in that certain way.
In the corridor she was about to enter her own room
again when she saw Fiona come out of Scott's consulting room. The practice manager raised her eyes
heavenwards when she caught sight of Olivia.

'Problems?' asked Olivia.

'I sometimes think my job description should include mother figure, agony aunt and confessor, along
with that of practice manager,' Fiona said.

'What's wrong?' Olivia glanced at Scott's closed
door.

'He's split up with Jane, his girlfriend,' Fiona murmured, following Olivia into her room. 'Wants me to
tell everyone—says he can't face it.'

'Well, I can't say I'm too surprised or, come to
that, particularly sorry,' said Olivia. 'I never did think
that young woman was right for Scott. Thoroughly
spoilt and too selfish for my liking.'

'My sentiments exactly,' replied Fiona firmly.

'How's he taking it?' Olivia frowned. She was fond
of Scott and didn't like to think of him suffering.

'Says he's depressed, but he'll get over it. It won't
take long for the girls to be after him, good-looking

young chap like that. And as for that lot in Reception, they'll be drooling when they know he's footloose and fancy-free again. Don't think I'll tell them yet. We won't get any work out of them when they find out.'

'I thought Brad was flavour of the month where they're concerned,' said Olivia with a wry chuckle.

'Oh, he was,' Fiona agreed. 'Until they realised they never stood a chance with him.'

'What do you mean?' Olivia had begun to sort out her case, ready to take on her house calls, but she paused and looked up curiously, wondering what the practice manager had meant. Fleetingly she even wondered whether Fiona had heard something about Brad that she, Olivia, didn't know. Something about his reason for leaving his last practice.

'Well, let's face it, Olivia,' said Fiona briskly, 'he does only have eyes for you, doesn't he?'

Olivia felt her cheeks redden. This was the second time such an observation had been made about Brad's supposed interest in her. First Alison and now Fiona. 'I don't know what you mean,' she said at last, returning to her case to cover her embarrassment.

'Oh, I think you do, Olivia,' said Fiona with a laugh. 'And if I were you, I'd just enjoy it. You haven't exactly overdosed on fun and romance in recent years, have you?'

'Well, no…'

'So this truly gorgeous man comes along and starts paying you a bit of attention… I ask you, those opportunities aren't exactly ten a penny, are they?'

'True,' Olivia agreed.

'And what about Hannah?'

'What *about* Hannah?'

'Well, does she like him?'

'As a matter of fact yes, she does...'

'Well, there you are, then. You're practically home and dry.'

'He takes an interest in her—that's why she likes him, and because he just happens to play the saxophone like a dream.'

'Gets more interesting by the minute.' Fiona laughed, but on turning to leave the room she said, 'Snap him up, Olivia. There can't be too many like him around.'

If only, thought Olivia as she stared at the closed door, it were that simple. But was she making difficulties where none existed? Because Brad happened to look like Danny Rickman it shouldn't automatically have influenced her feelings. And she didn't know for certain that Brad's decision to leave his last practice had had anything to do with another woman. As for him leaving to go to Canada in a few months' time...well, maybe she should forget about that, seize the moment, enjoy herself for once and hang the consequences. There would be time enough to worry about those if and when they materialised. And everyone seemed to be of the opinion that Brad was interested in her...

Her spirits lifting a little, she glanced out of the window and saw that for the first time in about a fortnight it had stopped raining. She finished packing her medical case then opened the door.

In Reception she found Brad already waiting for her. Mindful of her recent thoughts, she allowed her eyes to meet his, and when they did she smiled. For one moment he looked puzzled, as if he was unused to such a reaction from her, then his brow cleared and he smiled back, his expression implying that he couldn't quite believe his luck but that he intended making the most of the situation in case it changed again.

He automatically headed for his Range Rover and for once Olivia was content to let him take control. He still made her feel fragile and while before she had chafed against that feeling she found that now, for the time being at least, she was happy to go along with it and, indeed, even quite enjoyed it.

As Brad drove to the hospice they remained silent at first. It was as if both were somehow aware that something had changed between them but were afraid to say anything that might jeopardise this new-found congeniality.

In the end it was Brad who spoke. 'I think,' he said, 'this is the first time since coming to Malsonbury that I haven't had to use the windscreen wipers.'

'It doesn't always rain here,' Olivia replied. 'It really is quite a lovely place most of the time.'

'I don't doubt it.' Brad laughed. 'And I dare say it's the rain that makes it so beautiful in the long run.'

'Look…' Olivia pointed through the side window of the Range Rover. 'There's some blue sky up there and I do believe the sun is trying to come out.' In the distance a large patch of blue could be seen and the sun was, indeed, struggling through the thick grey cloud. 'It's incredible how a little sunshine transforms everything,' Olivia went on. 'Look at that mass of chrysanthemums in the flower-beds—I doubt we'd have even given them a second glance if it had still been raining, but you can't help but admire them with the sun on them.'

Brad nodded. 'I know what you mean. Even that copper beech looks as if it's glowing.'

'My mum loved copper beech,' said Olivia wistfully. 'It was her favourite tree. I always think of her whenever I see one.'

'You still miss her, don't you?' he said quietly as he drove into the grounds of the hospice.

'Yes, I do,' she agreed. 'She was a great force in my life.'

'In what way?' Brad threw her a curious glance as he switched off the engine.

'In making me believe I could still fulfil my ambitions even when all the odds were against it,' she replied. They both sat very still, neither of them making any attempt to get out of the vehicle.

'You mean because of Hannah?' he said at last.

She nodded. 'Yes, it was all incredibly difficult at the time, but it was my mum who made me see that it wasn't necessarily the end of the world, that I could still go to medical school and that I could still be a doctor in spite of my irresponsibility and the mistake I'd made. I was a year late, of course, because I had to wait until Hannah was a few months old, but I couldn't have done it without my mother, I'm well aware of that. My dad, too, really. They looked after Hannah for me, you see, while I did my training. I came home as often as I could but they carried the brunt of it.'

'And what about Hannah's father? Couldn't he have helped at all?'

Olivia stiffened instinctively at the mention of Danny but realised it was inevitable that Brad would be curious—anyone would, really. 'No,' she said, at last, 'he didn't help. He couldn't, really...'

'Was he married?' he asked softly.

'No, no,' she said, 'he wasn't married. At least not at first…'

When Olivia lapsed into silence, he said, 'I'm sorry. I didn't mean to pry.'

'No,' she said quickly, 'it's all right. Really it is. It's just something I haven't talked about much, that's all. The fact is, Hannah's father couldn't really help because he never knew about her.' As Brad sharply drew in his breath she went on, 'I should have told him, I know, but my parents—my mother especially—persuaded me not to. She said it was far better to leave matters as they were. I think she thought I might go off with Danny and then all my dreams of being a doctor would have gone out of the window.'

'Hmm,' said Brad.

'I suppose it was wrong,' said Olivia. 'He worked for a travelling funfair and I don't think he earned very much. I never wrote and told him when I found I was pregnant. Oh, I had written to him before, of course, when the fair had first moved on, but he'd never bothered to reply. I can't for one moment imagine he would have been exactly thrilled to learn of my condition.'

'And was that it? Did you never see him again?'

Olivia hesitated. Taking a deep breath she said, 'Oh, yes, I saw him once more. It was when Hannah was about two years old. I was at medical school and I heard that the same fair was visiting a town a few miles away. I decided to go there. I don't know why, I suppose I just wanted to see if Danny was still with the fair.'

'Did you take Hannah with you?'

'No, nothing like that. She was at home with my

parents. I didn't know what I was going to do if I did see Danny. Maybe I had some silly notion that if I confronted him with the facts he would want me...and his daughter... I don't know.' She gave a helpless little gesture with her hands.

'You loved him,' said Brad.

'Oh, yes, I loved him. I loved him so much it hurt,' said Olivia with a wry smile. 'First love and all that...'

'So was he still there? Did you see him?'

'Yes, he was there, I saw him. I made enquiries at the change kiosk and the boy there told me that, yes, Danny was still with them. When I asked where I could find him I was directed to a rather run-down caravan at the far side of the field. Luckily, before I had a chance to knock at the door and make a complete and utter fool of myself he came out of the caravan. I managed to conceal myself and it was fortunate I did because Danny wasn't alone—he had a heavily pregnant young girl with him and in his arms he carried a small boy of about eighteen months.'

'He didn't waste any time, did he?' said Brad softly. He paused. 'So how did all that make you feel?'

'I felt dreadful at first,' Olivia admitted, 'but I soon got over that. In fact, after that I rapidly got over Danny. Seeing that girl, I had a glimpse of what my life would have been like had I gone with him—travelling from town to town, a baby every year...' She shrugged. 'It might have been tough for me at times, bringing up Hannah, but it hasn't been that tough.' She was silent for a moment, reflecting on what might have been, then she gave a little shiver. 'Come on,' she said, 'we'd better get on.'

'Yes.' He nodded, and as she turned to open her door he said, 'Thanks for telling me, Olivia.'

'That's OK. I just felt I wanted you to know. I wanted to set the record straight, if you like.'

They entered the hospice in silence, but it was a companionable silence. It was as if in the last hour they'd reached a new level of understanding.

While Brad went off with Matron to see Stephen Trowbridge a staff nurse took Olivia to Grace Hawkins's room.

Grace's family was still gathered around her bed — her two daughters, a granddaughter and a niece. On seeing Olivia, they made as if to leave.

'No, please, don't feel you have to go,' said Olivia quickly. 'I won't be long.' After setting down her case, she carefully carried out the necessary procedures to check that life was no longer present, that the patient no longer had pulse or heartbeat, that breathing had ceased and that the pupils were fixed and dilated.

'She seemed very peaceful at the end, Doctor,' said Grace's elder daughter. 'I don't think she was in any pain.'

'I'm sure she wasn't,' Olivia replied. 'The staff made sure her pain was very well controlled.'

'They have been marvellous here,' said the other daughter. 'I never realised before what a wonderful job the hospice movement does. Mum was really worried about coming here but I can honestly say that after a few days she was content and she just seemed to stop worrying about everything.'

'Look at her skin,' said Grace's granddaughter wonderingly. 'She looks like a young girl now, it's so smooth.'

'I'd like to thank you, Dr Chandler,' said the elder daughter to Olivia, 'for all your kindness and attention to Mum.'

'It's been a pleasure,' replied Olivia quietly. 'She was a lovely lady.'

She left shortly after that. After going to Matron's office and signing the death certificate for Grace, she went into the hall to wait for Brad.

'Have you come to see the lad?'

She had been admiring an arrangement of late roses in a vase on the sideboard but she turned at the voice, to find old Samuel Leigh at her elbow. 'I'm sorry?' she said.

'The boy…Stephen Trowbridge. Have you come to see him? You're the doctor who came before, aren't you?' He glared at her, his eyes burning fiercely in his emaciated face.

'Yes, I am. But another doctor is seeing Stephen today—Dr Bradley.'

'Well let's hope he knows his stuff,' said Samuel, 'because that lad isn't well. He isn't well at all, I tell you. Something should be done about it and that's a fact. You expect it with an old codger like me—I've had my life and a good one it's been and all—but a young whippersnapper like that? No, I tell you. Something must be done.'

Olivia took a deep breath. 'I assure you, Mr Leigh,' she said, 'everything will be done for Stephen that can be done.'

'Yes, well, you just make sure it is, that's all.' With that Samuel turned on his heel and stomped off down the corridor to his room.

A few minutes later Olivia was joined by Brad and

Matron. One look at their faces told Olivia that old Samuel's fear had not been unfounded.

'How is he?' she asked.

'His blood count is very low,' Brad replied. 'I'm having him admitted to the General.' He turned to Matron. 'The ambulance should be here shortly.'

'Thank you, Dr Bradley,' Matron replied. 'I've sent for Stephen's mother and she's on her way.'

'Is there a father?' asked Olivia quickly.

'They're divorced,' Matron replied. 'He works abroad.'

'We'll keep in touch with the hospital,' said Brad.

'Good. Well, thank you both once again,' said Matron crisply as she escorted them to the front door.

Moments later they were driving out of the grounds of the hospice. 'It's like another world in there,' said Olivia with a sigh as they drove through the gates. With a quick glance at Brad's set profile she said, 'What did you think of Stephen?'

'I didn't like the look of him.' Brad shook his head. 'He'll need a blood transfusion.'

'Poor lad,' said Olivia softly. As Brad drew out into the traffic she added, 'Apparently he knows Hannah. Or so he told me the last time I saw him.'

'From school?'

'No. Hannah's at an all-girls' school and, besides, he's a fair bit older than her. He said his friend Damon likes Hannah and that they know each other from the youth club. Funny thing is, I've never heard Hannah mention either of them.'

'Did you always mention the boys you knew to your parents?'

'No, I guess not,' she replied with a laugh, on re-

flection adding, 'Definitely not where Danny was concerned—at least until I had to.'

'Well, there you are, then.'

'How about you?' she asked after a moment.

'Me?' He sounded surprised that she should ask.

'Yes. Did you always tell your mum about your
girlfriends?'

When he didn't immediately answer she threw him
a sideways look, and was dismayed to see that shadowed look of sadness on his face she'd seen there
before. Before she had a chance to say anything further he spoke.

'There weren't that many,' he said at last. 'Just one
really.'

'Oh.' For a moment she was lost for words. This
wasn't what she'd imagined at all. 'And now?' she
dared to ask at last.

He shook his head. 'No, there's no one now.'

When next she brought herself to look at him the
shadowed look had gone and he was his old self
again.

Whoever she was, it seemed she'd hurt him very
badly if she was responsible for that expression of
sadness. Quite suddenly Olivia felt angry at this
unknown woman and unexpectedly protective towards Brad.

# CHAPTER NINE

A PHONE was ringing somewhere—not Olivia's phone, it was further away than that. Nevertheless, she struggled up from the depths of sleep as she had trained and disciplined herself to do over the years. Her bedside clock told her it was two-thirty and as her brain cleared she realised it must have been Brad's phone she'd heard in the flat next door, and she remembered he was on call.

Slipping out of bed, she padded to the loo, wondering if she could get back to bed without fully waking up. As she passed Hannah's room on her return something prompted her to look inside. She didn't know why she did so because it certainly wasn't something she made a habit of doing in the middle of the night. Later she was to wonder if it had been maternal intuition which had prompted her action, but at the time all she was aware of was standing in the doorway and staring in stupefaction at her daughter's empty bed.

It took only a moment for her brain to slip into gear and for her to be galvanised into action. After she'd satisfied herself that Hannah was nowhere in the house she hurried outside and knocked on the door of the flat. There was a light on upstairs and when, a few moments later, the door swung open she wasn't surprised to see that Brad was fully dressed in a thick, polo-necked sweater and dark cords.

'Olivia! What is it?' He looked both surprised to

see her at that hour and concerned as to what might have brought her there.

'It's Hannah,' she said, coming straight to the point. 'She isn't in her bed…and she's nowhere in the house. I'm sorry.' She paused. 'You have to go out. I just wasn't sure what to do for the moment. It seems silly, calling the police, until I actually know she's missing…'

Suddenly in the light from the lamp over the door she realised that Brad was staring at her in a strange way. 'What is it?' she asked hesitantly. 'What's wrong?'

'Nothing,' he said quickly. 'Now, you musn't get alarmed, but I think I know where Hannah might be.'

'What do you mean?' She stared back at him. Her heart had given a painful lurch at his words.

'The call I've had,' he explained, 'is to a barn out on the Chippenham road. Some kids are having a rave…'

'She wouldn't!' Olivia's hand flew to her mouth. 'I'd forgotten that was tonight. But she told me she didn't want to go…'

'Bit of a coincidence, don't you think?' Brad raised his eyebrows.

'Why have you been called?' Olivia demanded.

'It was the police who called me,' he replied. 'Something to do with drugs. A girl has been taken ill…'

Olivia stared at him, aghast.

'I'm coming with you,' she said abruptly at last. 'Give me a minute.' Not giving him a chance to argue, she dashed back into the house where she ripped off her dressing-gown, pulled on her trench coat over her pyjamas, kicked off her slippers and thrust her feet into a pair of boots.

Moments later they were in the Range Rover and Brad was reversing out of the square.

'I can't believe she's done this,' muttered Olivia as they drove through the night.

'Don't be too hard on her,' murmured Brad.

'Hard on her?' said Olivia incredulously. 'Honestly, I could kill her!'

'Come on, Olivia,' he said soothingly. 'You don't mean that.'

'Don't I?' she said. 'Just you watch me!'

'Cast your mind back to when you were her age.'

'If I'd done this when I was her age,' said Olivia through gritted teeth, 'my father *would* have killed me. There's no two ways about it.'

Theirs was the only vehicle on the road as they travelled for several miles into the windswept countryside. They passed a public house, all in darkness, its sign swinging eerily in the wind. Brad peered through the windscreen and took a sharp left turn into a narrow lane with tall hedges on either side.

'Do you know exactly where this barn is?' he asked a few moments later.

'Not really.' Olivia shook her head. 'I just know it's somewhere in this area. It probably isn't even visible from the road. What exactly did the police say?'

'Not a lot. Just that it's well off the beaten track, that I had to turn left at the pub then it's about two miles further on down the lane. Apparently there's a path across the fields.'

'How did she get here, for goodness' sake?' muttered Olivia as she gnawed anxiously at her thumb-nail.

'Do any of her friends drive?' asked Brad.

'Not that I know of—they're all far too young.'

'Someone must have given her a lift.'

They fell silent again for a while as all sorts of irrational thoughts flashed through Olivia's mind—Hannah as a baby, lifting her arms to be picked up, as a toddler, playing in her paddling pool, later with her clarinet in the orchestra, and recently, and more disturbingly, in her short skirt with her long legs in Lycra tights and her hair tumbling about her shoulders. Other images flashed unbidden into her mind—Hannah high on drugs, Hannah with a gang of leather-clad youths, Hannah lying cold in a ditch, her face swollen, her lips blue...

'What did the police say about drugs?' she demanded, turning to Brad at last in growing desperation.

'Simply that one girl had been taken ill,' he replied, his voice calm and reassuring as if he sensed her growing hysteria. 'I guess they must have raided the place, suspecting drugs were being used.'

'Oh, my God,' she whispered. 'It'll be Hannah... I just know it...'

'Now, you don't know that,' he replied in the same calm tones. 'Come to that, we don't even know for sure that this is where she is.'

'Well, where else would she be?' Olivia's voice was shrill with worry.

'Damn, it's raining again—that's all we need!' Brad leaned forward, peering through the windscreen. 'Now we have to turn off somewhere along here. It's an unadopted track apparently. I hope I haven't missed it. The police said about two miles from the main road and I guess we've done that.'

'Wait!' cried Olivia suddenly. 'I think that might have been it! Back there.'

Brad braked sharply then reversed back a few yards to where a single track fell away between thick hedges. 'Yes,' he muttered, 'I think you're right.'

The Range Rover bumped down a track deeply rutted because of the amount of recent rain. Once or twice the wheels began to spin in the mud but the Range Rover held the ground well and a few minutes later the hedges thinned out. In the distance across fields, against the lighter sky, they could see the dark outline of a large barn and in front of that the rotating blue lights of police vehicles.

'That's it!' breathed Olivia.

The path across the fields was churned up by the recent passage of many vehicles, and as they slowly approached the barn it seemed as if the whole building was vibrating. Olivia wound down the window and they could hear the steady thump, thump of the music.

A policeman, waving a torch, came to meet them. 'Dr Bradley?' he said as Brad wound down his window.

Brad nodded. 'Yes, and this is my colleague, Dr Chandler,' he replied.

'Perhaps you'd like to park up over there.' The policeman pointed towards one side of the barn. 'It's a little less muddy there. The kids have parked their vehicles on the far side. It's like a quagmire over there—it's going to be a devil of a job, getting them out.'

Brad parked the Range Rover and he and Olivia

got out, Brad retrieving his medical case from the rear seat.

'This way, Doctor.' The policeman led the way through the huge doors to the interior of the barn.

Olivia wasn't quite sure what she'd been expecting, but the sight that met her eyes caused her to stop and stare in amazement. The whole place was heaving, a throbbing mass of writhing, gyrating bodies. Strobe lighting had been erected on the wooden beams and the supports of the barn, and the resulting flickering light gave a slightly surreal effect, reminiscent of an old-time Hollywood movie.

Some youngsters, scantily clad in unbuttoned shirts, waved bottles as they danced, taking an occasional swig. Others, boys and girls alike, punched the air repeatedly in frenetic gestures. Most were dripping in sweat, and all ignored the presence of the police and the two doctors.

'Where's the girl?' yelled Brad against the din.

It was doubtful whether the policeman heard him but he must have anticipated the question because he raised one arm, his gesture indicating that Brad and Olivia should follow him. He led them to a far corner of the barn behind stacked bales of hay, which seemed to serve as something of a buffer to the sound. There was someone lying on the ground and as Olivia approached a terrible sense of foreboding swept over her and she could hardly bring herself to look at the pathetic little bundle. A policewoman was crouching on the ground and had covered the girl with her jacket.

As Brad sank to his knees beside the figure Olivia steeled herself to look. The girl was lying on her side, her hair partly obscuring her face which, even in that subdued lighting, looked deathly pale, her eyes closed. While Olivia was trying to absorb the fact that this girl had dark hair so she couldn't therefore be Hannah, there was a movement on the other side of the policewoman and another figure appeared. The next moment Olivia was staring into the horror-filled gaze of her daughter.

'Hannah!' she gasped.

'Mum. Oh, Mum!' Hannah flung herself into Olivia's arms and for a split second Olivia forgot everything else in the realisation that her daughter was safe. Briefly she held Hannah away from her and her gaze flew once more to the girl on the ground. Brad had now turned her onto her back, and with sudden shock she realised it was Charlotte.

'Is she dead?' Frantically Hannah clung to Olivia.

Brad looked up and shook his head. 'No, she's unconscious. What has she taken, Hannah?'

Hannah didn't reply, gazing instead down at her friend with terror in her eyes.

'We need to know,' shouted Brad above the throb of the music.

Taking Hannah by the arm, Olivia propelled her towards an open doorway at the rear of the barn and outside into the damp night air. The shock of the sudden change of atmosphere seemed to hit Hannah, and within seconds she was shaking and had started to cry. Carefully Olivia shut the door behind them, blotting out at least some of the deafening noise inside. Taking Hannah by the shoulders, she turned her daughter to face her.

'Hannah,' she said, 'we have to know if we are going to help Charlotte. What has she taken?'

By this time Hannah's teeth were chattering and

Olivia feared she was going into shock. She was on the point of despairing of getting the information they needed out of her daughter when at that moment the door opened behind them and a boy slipped out of the barn and shut the door behind him.

'Are you OK, Hannah?' he said.

Hannah nodded. 'It's my...my...m-mum,' she stuttered.

'Who are you?' Olivia rounded on the boy who, on closer scrutiny, looked older than she had at first thought.

'I'm...I'm Hannah's boyfriend.'

Olivia stared at the boy as somewhere in her brain a bell sounded.

'Oh, are you?' she said. 'Well, I'm her mother and I just happen to be a doctor, so maybe you can tell us what Charlotte has taken. We'll find out eventually because I'm sure the police will be carrying out a thorough search, but by then it may be too late to save Charlotte's life so you may as well tell me now.'

Hannah gave a little whimper and Olivia saw fear flicker in the boy's eyes. He glanced once at Hannah. 'Ecstasy,' he said at last. 'That's what she took.'

'How many?' demanded Olivia.

'Just the one as far as I know.'

'Right. Back inside, you two.' Olivia tugged open the door and strode into the barn again. Brad was still on the floor beside the unconscious form of Charlotte. His questioning gaze met Olivia's.

'Ecstasy,' she mouthed. 'One, we think.'

Brad nodded and began rummaging in his bag. Olivia knelt beside him so that she could hear what he was saying. 'Her airway's clear but she'll be dehydrated,' he said. 'I'm going to put a drip up.' He took a bag of Haemaccel from his case which Olivia held while he inserted a cannula in the back of Charlotte's hand. In seconds the life-saving fluid was dripping into her vein.

'Do you want us to radio for an ambulance?' asked the policeman as he crouched beside them.

'It'll take some time for an ambulance to get out here,' said Brad. 'I think we'll take her to hospital ourselves. It'll be faster in the long run.'

'Did you say it was Ecstasy she'd taken?' The policeman stood up.

Olivia nodded. 'Just the one, apparently, but you can be sure there are more in there.' She jerked her head in the direction of the main section of the barn.

'Yes, we know,' shouted the policeman. 'We've prevented anyone from leaving and we've got reinforcements coming. As soon as they arrive we'll put a stop to this lot and do a thorough search.' Even as he spoke the wail of police sirens could be heard above the music. Moments later the music screeched to a shuddering stop as dozens of uniformed police swarmed into the barn.

'Can my daughter come with us?' asked Olivia.

'When she's been searched.' The policeman looked at the WPC and nodded. She stood up and walked across to Hannah.

'Do you have any drugs on you?' she asked.

Hannah shook her head.

'Have you taken any tonight?'

Olivia found herself holding her breath as she waited for her daughter's reply. As Hannah shook her head again Olivia breathed a sigh of relief. It didn't take the WPC long to search Hannah as all she was wearing was a skimpy red top Olivia couldn't remember having seen before, and which barely covered her midriff, and the shortest of skirts.

'Right, you can go with your mother, young lady,' said the policeman after a nod from the WPC, 'but we may want to see you tomorrow down at the station to answer further questions.'

'I'm going to carry Charlotte outside now,' said Brad as he closed his case. 'Olivia, can you hold the drip and bring my case, please?'

As Hannah stood there, with tears running down her cheeks, the boy was propelled away by the policeman into the main body of the barn to join all the other young people, quiet and subdued now as they waited to be questioned. Brad crouched down and gently eased Charlotte into his arms.

'Come on, Hannah,' said Olivia sharply, jerking her daughter from the stupor she seemed to have slipped into. Together they made their way outside to the waiting Range Rover.

On the drive back to Malsonbury Olivia was amazed to find that the rear of Brad's Range Rover was equipped like the vehicle of a paramedic, and that with a little adaptation of the seats Charlotte was able to lie flat as if she were on a couch. While Brad drove and Hannah sat beside him in the front passenger seat, Olivia kept a close watch on Charlotte, frequently checking that the drip was working correctly and that her pulse and blood pressure remained steady.

Brad drove directly to the town's general hospital, having telephoned ahead on his mobile phone to give details of the patient and their expected time of arrival. As they swung into the grounds of the hospital and came to a halt in a bay beside the accident and emergency wing, they were met by a doctor, a casualty nurse and two other members of staff with a stretcher trolley.

After Brad and Olivia had given further details of Charlotte's condition to the staff, they were forced to stand back as she was wheeled speedily away.

'What do we do now?' asked Hannah in a small voice.

'We wait,' said Brad, 'until they can tell us a little more about her condition.'

'I need to phone her mother,' said Olivia. 'I told the police I would. I imagine this is going to be as big a shock for her as it was for me when I found your bed empty.' She looked at Hannah, who hung her head.

'Do you want to use my mobile?' asked Brad.

'No, thanks all the same. I'll use the phone in Reception.'

'In that case, I think I'll get a hot, sweet drink for this young lady,' said Brad, putting one arm around Hannah's shoulders, 'and see if we can stop this shaking.'

'Thanks, Brad.' Olivia flashed him a grateful glance then hurried ahead into the casualty reception area to carry out her unenviable task.

The phone was answered on the fifteenth ring. 'Hello?' The voice, although sleepy, was unmistakably that of Frances Blake.

'Frances, it's Olivia Chandler.'

'Olivia?' The surprise in the single word was evident.

'Yes, I'm sorry to haul you out of bed like this, Frances, but I'm afraid I have some upsetting news for you. I'm at the General Hospital. I've just helped Dr Bradley to bring Charlotte into Casualty...'

'Charlotte?' Frances sounded incredulous now. 'You can't have. Charlotte's asleep upstairs in bed.'

'No, Frances, she isn't. She's here in the hospital. She and Hannah went to that rave party and, well, there's been an incident and I think you should come down to the hospital right away—'

'Wait a minute, Olivia. Hold on, please…'

Olivia, knowing how confused and disbelieving Frances was feeling, waited patiently while she, no doubt, went upstairs to check. She was back within a few minutes.

'Olivia…you were right! Her bed hasn't even been slept in. I can't believe it—' At that point the phone was apparently taken away from her and Olivia heard Geoffrey's voice still thick from sleep.

'What's happened to her, Olivia?' he asked.

'She was given some sort of drugs—Ecstasy, we think. She collapsed, Geoffrey. She's unconscious…'

'We're on our way, Olivia.' The line went dead. Olivia hung up and made her way back to the waiting area where Brad and Hannah were sipping tea from white plastic cups. Brad handed one to her.

'Thanks,' she said curling her hands around the cup and drawing comfort from its warmth.

'Thought you might be in need of that,' said Brad quietly.

Olivia sipped her tea and looked at Hannah. She was glad to see that her daughter's shaking was subsiding, but she looked terrible, with dark circles around her eyes and her hair hanging limply round her white face.

They sat in silence until Frances and Geoffrey arrived. They both looked distraught and sick with anxiety, Frances with her black hair screwed back from her face and fastened with a slide and her husband wearing odd shoes so great had been his haste. While Geoffrey took himself off to enquire about his daughter, Olivia and Brad attempted to console Frances.

'We'd forbidden her to go,' said Frances, looking at Hannah. 'I can't believe she did it. Geoffrey said there would be drugs there. Were you with her, Hannah?' she demanded suddenly, as if the thought had only just occurred to her.

'Yes.' Hannah gulped then nodded.

'But I thought you'd been forbidden to go as well.' Frances looked wildly at Olivia.

'No,' she said quietly. 'I didn't forbid Hannah because she'd already told me she didn't want to go.'

'Who gave her the drugs? Come on,' Frances went on urgently when Hannah remained silent, 'if you were there you must have known—'

'I think it's best to leave that for the moment,' said Brad quietly. 'Hannah's had a shock as well. No doubt the police will get to the bottom of things and find out who was responsible for supplying the drugs.'

'The police?' Frances looked bewildered. 'Are they involved as well?'

'Yes, it was the police who called me out,' said Brad. As Frances gave him a blank look he explained, 'I'm Dr Bradley. I'm a locum at Olivia's practice.'

At that moment Geoffrey returned. 'They say she's still unconscious but that we can go and see her now,' he said, taking his wife's arm.

'Frances, is there anything you'd like me to do?' asked Olivia. When Frances looked blankly at her, she went on, 'What about Thomas? Is he on his own?'

'No.' Frances shook her head. 'My mother is staying with us. She woke up when the phone rang. She knows we've come here.'

'In that case we'll go home, but I'll be in touch, Frances.'

Frances nodded vaguely and her husband led her away, but as they reached the double doors that led from Reception into the accident and emergency treatment rooms he paused and looked back at Olivia and Brad. 'Thank you,' he said, 'for all you've done tonight.'

After the Blakes had disappeared from sight Brad looked at Olivia. 'Before we go,' he said, 'I'll go and see if I can get any update on Charlotte.'

When Brad had gone Olivia and Hannah sat together in silence, each lost in her own thoughts. Olivia still felt stunned by the events of the night and could identify entirely with Frances's bewilderment. Turning her head briefly, she was in time to see two large tears spill from Hannah's eyes and run down her cheeks. Instinctively she put her arms around her daughter and drew her close.

'Oh, Mum,' Hannah choked. 'What if she dies? Whatever will I do?'

'Come on, Hannah. Don't think like that. Charlotte's in the best place now and she'll get the best treatment.' Olivia smoothed Hannah's hair out of her eyes then looked up quickly as Brad reappeared. 'Any news?' she said quickly.

'I've spoken to the registrar,' he replied. 'They are going to give her a brain scan.'

'Oh, no,' whimpered Hannah.

'It's just a precautionary measure to make sure there isn't any permanent damage,' said Brad hurriedly as he caught sight of Hannah's tears.

'I think we'd better get home,' said Olivia, rising to her feet.

'Good idea,' said Brad. 'We can't do any more here tonight—and this young lady looks exhausted,' he added as he put his arm across Hannah's shoulders.

Together the three of them made their way out of the hospital and into the waiting Range Rover. Minutes later as the first light of dawn was touching the morning sky Brad drove them back to the house in the square.

# CHAPTER TEN

HANNAH seemed on the brink of exhaustion and when they went indoors Olivia took her straight up the stairs to bed.

'I won't be long,' she said to Brad over the bannisters. 'I expect you'll be wanting to get to bed as well.'

'Actually, I'm wide awake now.'

'Me, too,' she admitted.

'In that case, shall I put the kettle on?'

'Good idea.'

In Hannah's bedroom Olivia helped her daughter to undress, drawing the skimpy little top over her head and slipping her nightshirt over the mass of her hair just as she'd been accustomed to doing when Hannah had been a little girl, the only difference being that then she'd smelt of baby shampoo and warm milk and now she smelt of cigarette smoke and alcohol.

'Mum, I'm sorry,' Hannah whispered as Olivia helped her into bed and pulled up the duvet. Already her eyes, smudged with mascara, were beginning to close.

'We'll talk about it later,' said Olivia gently but firmly.

'That boy…'

'Boy?'

'The one I was with…'

'Damon?'

138

'How did you know…that was his name?'

'I just knew. Now sleep, and, as I said, we'll talk later…'

But Hannah's eyes were closed by then and Olivia doubted whether she'd even heard her. For a moment she stared down at her daughter and her heart wrenched in her chest as she thought of the events of the night. Gently she leaned forward and kissed the smooth, peach-like skin of Hannah's cheek. She stood up and, moving to the door, switched off the light. She stood for another moment, watching her sleeping daughter, then left the room and wearily went back down the stairs.

She found Brad in the kitchen. He looked up quickly as she entered the room, his gaze seeking hers.

'Is she all right?' he said.

Olivia nodded and, sinking down onto a chair, briefly held her head in her hands. 'She's asleep,' she said simply.

'Good.' He paused. 'I thought tea and toast might be in order—it is, after all, nearly six-thirty.'

'Where did the night go?' she murmured, watching him as he transferred hot slices of toast from the toaster to a plate in the centre of the table then poured tea from her big earthenware teapot into two mugs.

They were silent for a while and to her surprise Olivia found she was hungry.

'I didn't imagine I could eat anything when you mentioned food,' she said, buttering her second slice of toast, 'and now just look at me.'

'You've burnt up a lot of reserve energy tonight,' said Brad, topping up the tea in his mug.

With a sigh Olivia sat back in her chair. 'What am

I going to do with her, Brad?' she asked, and her voice sounded close to despair. 'How do I handle this?'

He looked thoughtful as he stirred his tea. 'You may find,' he said at last, 'that the shock element of tonight's proceedings will be all that's needed to bring her to her senses.'

'If anything happens to Charlotte, God knows what it will do to Hannah. The pair of them have been inseparable since they were toddlers.'

'I think she'll pull through all right, but the worrying thing is how long she's unconscious.'

'I know. The thought of brain damage…' Olivia trailed off helplessly.

'Has Hannah ever done anything like this before?' he asked a moment later.

Olivia shook her head. 'No, nothing. Oh, there've been the usual things, but nothing this bad. I still can hardly believe she did it. Sneaking out in the middle of the night, that's bad enough… But being involved in drugs…and the police! The trouble is…I blame myself…'

'It's hardly your fault,' Brad protested mildly.

'I should have suspected something. She changed her mind too easily. She was desperate to go one minute then the next she was saying she wasn't interested, that she didn't want to go. I should have been suspicious. As it was, I was simply relieved that I didn't have another battle on my hands. Little did I know…'

'You still can't take the blame—'

'And then there was that boy,' she interrupted Brad, as if she hadn't heard him.

'The boy she was with? Did you know him?' He frowned.

'No. I didn't know him, and that's the whole point.
I should have done. I should have known who
Hannah's friends were. To make matters worse, I
knew *of* him. You remember the first day you were
here and we went to the hospice?' Brad nodded and
she continued, 'Well, Stephen Trowbridge asked me
if I was Hannah Chandler's mother. When I asked
him how he knew her he said he'd met her at the
youth club and that his friend Damon liked her. I
should have asked Hannah about this Damon straight
away, but I didn't.'

'And that was Damon with her tonight?'

'Yes, I just mentioned him to her and she was surprised I knew his name. I should have pursued it before, Brad. For a start he's a fair bit older than her.'

'You weren't to know that.'

'I should have done. I knew Stephen was around
seventeen—it stands to reason his friend would probably be about the same age.'

'Has Hannah had boyfriends in the past?' asked
Brad slowly.

'Yes, but only boys from the local school. They
would go to school discos, that sort of thing. They
were always about the same age as her.'

'She does look older...*I* thought she was older
when I first met her.'

'And maybe I'm to blame for that as well,' said
Olivia bitterly.

'How can you be?' He sounded faintly incredulous
that she should even suggest it.

'I don't know...' She waved her hand dismissively.
'Maybe I should have supervised her clothes, her hair-
style and her make-up a bit more than I did...'

'Well, I don't know a lot about teenage girls,' said

Brad, 'but I would say that what you're suggesting is pretty well impossible.'

'Maybe—I don't know.' With a shrug Olivia pushed her plate away. 'All I do know,' she said, 'is that I have a real problem on my hands now. And I guess I have to be careful which way I handle it. She's very headstrong, Brad, and if I come down too hard on her she could fly off at a tangent. On the other hand, I can't let her get away with it or she'll walk all over me in the future and think she can get all her own way.'

'Why don't you go and see if you can get some rest for a couple of hours?' he said, and the concern in his voice was only too apparent.

'I don't think there's a lot of point. I'm too keyed up. I wouldn't be able to sleep.'

'Maybe this will help.' He stood up and moved round the table until he was standing behind her chair.

Olivia felt herself tense, anticipating what was coming. She felt his hands on her shoulders, his thumbs seeking and finding the knotted muscles at the base of her neck. And then, just as before on that other occasion at the surgery, she felt herself slowly begin to relax as his hands once again performed their magic.

She wasn't sure how long she sat there as all the pent-up tension of the night melted away until at last he stopped the rhythmic motion of his hands and dropped a kiss on the nape of her neck. 'Maybe now you'll be able to rest,' he whispered, leaning forward until his mouth was against her hair.

Somehow, and afterwards she wasn't even sure how it had happened, his arms went around her. She twisted her body and as his lips found hers her own arms slid around his neck.

The kiss was gentle but at the same time deeply satisfying, almost as if she had been anticipating it and waiting for it from the very moment they'd met. Neither was she disappointed for while it bore no resemblance to what she remembered of Danny's kisses it held a fire of its own and hinted at a deeper passion.

At last they drew apart and Olivia rose shakily to her feet. 'I'm not sure we should have done that,' she said, her voice husky.

'Why not?' he said softly. 'It just seemed natural...and inevitable. And after all, it hurts no one.'

Only me, she thought as a few moments later Brad went back to his flat to get some rest and she wearily made her way up the stairs. She would be the only one liable to be hurt if she got too fond of him and then he took himself off to Canada, going out of her life just as Danny had done all those years ago.

She glanced in at Hannah as she passed her door and was relieved to find that her daughter still slept. Once in her own room she slipped beneath her duvet. At first she thought she might simply drop off to sleep, but while Brad's massage had relaxed her almost to a state of oblivion his kiss had set her pulse racing and she found sleep eluded her because she could think of nothing else.

She must have slept at last from sheer exhaustion because when next she opened her eyes it was bright daylight. Sunshine streamed into her bedroom and the hands of her clock stood at ten o'clock. With a start she sat up, thinking for one dreadful moment that she was late for surgery. In the split second before she recalled the dreadful events of the night she remembered first that it was Sunday and then that Brad had kissed her.

For some time she lay there, trying to get her thoughts into some sort of order, wondering about Charlotte and about how she should handle the situation with Hannah. And then, inevitably, her thoughts turned to Brad and she found herself wondering what would happen next, quite where they went from there. Both of them knew that their relationship had changed now, not only because of the kiss they'd shared but also because of the events that had led up to it. Possibly to some people a single kiss would have meant very little, but deep in her heart Olivia knew that wouldn't be the case for Brad and herself.

With a sigh she slipped out of bed and padded across the floor to the shower room.

It was lunchtime before Hannah emerged, and by then Olivia had phoned the hospital for news of Charlotte.

'What did they say?' demanded Hannah. 'How is she?'

'Well, she's regained consciousness,' Olivia replied.

'Thank God for that…'

'But she's not out of the wood yet. There's still a chance there may be some degree of brain damage. They have to carry out more tests this morning. Oh, and the police phoned.'

Hannah had been about to make herself some toast but she stopped and threw Olivia a startled glance. 'What did they say?' she asked fearfully. 'Do I have to go down to the station?'

'No, they said not…'

Hannah visibly sagged with relief.

'They were satisfied that you weren't in possession of drugs.' Olivia paused and there was silence in the large kitchen. 'Apparently, though, there were several others there who were, and who have been arrested and charged.'

Hannah stayed silent. She carried her plate of toast to the table and sat down. She still looked pale, tired and very drawn.

'We have to talk, Hannah,' said Olivia quietly at last, and her daughter raised her dark eyes to her, so like Danny's.

'What about?' she said, and there was rebellion now in her stare, as if sleep had fortified her and the terrified child of the previous night had disappeared and been replaced.

'What about?' Olivia almost exploded, then checked herself and in a more restrained tone said, 'I would say, Hannah, there's plenty we need to talk about. Damon for a start—and before you ask I only know about him because a friend of his happens to be a patient of mine.'

Hannah stared at her. 'I suppose you mean Stephen,' she muttered. When Olivia didn't reply she shrugged, knowing better than to question her mother about a patient.

'So where did you meet him?'

'At the youth club.'

'Did you go out with him other than when you saw him at the youth club?'

'A few times,' Hannah admitted. 'It was no big deal.'

'Where did I think you were?'

'At Charlotte's. She was going out with one of Damon's friends.'

'And I suppose Charlotte's mother thought she was here. Is that right, Hannah? Hannah?' She spoke more sharply when Hannah made no attempt to answer.

'Yes, I guess so,' Hannah replied at last with a shrug.

'Why didn't you feel able to tell me where you were going?'

Hannah shrugged again. 'Knew you wouldn't like it, I suppose.'

'Knew I wouldn't like what?' Olivia paused, waiting for some further response, but Hannah remained with her eyes downcast, staring at the table. 'Was it Damon you thought I wouldn't like? Was that it? Was it because he's much older than you?'

'He's not *that* much older!' Hannah protested, stung to a retort. 'He's only seventeen, for heaven's sake!'

'And that's three years older than you. Was that why you didn't say anything?' Olivia persisted.

'Yes, if you must know.' Hannah looked up then, her eyes flashing. 'I didn't tell you because I knew you'd go on like this. I knew there would be a lot of hassle about nothing! I knew if I said anything you would go on and on about homework and A levels. You'd have stopped me going to the youth club and you'd have tried to stop me from seeing Damon.'

'I would certainly wanted to have met him first,' Olivia replied, trying to keep her voice measured and under control. 'I've told you time and again, Hannah, I want to know where you are at all times and I want to know who you are with. And I've always encouraged you to bring your friends home…'

'Even if I had, you'd have objected to Damon—I know you would.'

'Why? What is there about him that I would have objected to, apart from his age? Is he into drugs?'

'No!' Hannah's answer was instant and emphatic. 'He doesn't take drugs.'

'So who gave Charlotte the Ecstasy? Someone gave it to her, Hannah. Was it the boy she's been going out with?'

Hannah looked at the table again. 'No, she's finished with him. It was another guy,' she muttered at last. 'He told Charlotte she'd have a great time and that there wasn't any harm in it. I told her not to, but she wouldn't listen. She liked this guy, you see. She was hoping he'd ask her out.'

'And had she met him at the youth club as well?'

'He used to hang about there,' Hannah admitted at last.

'No doubt hoping to lure silly little girls into drug-taking and heaven only knows what else. Honestly, Hannah, don't you realise Charlotte could have died last night? Probably very nearly did. She could still have suffered permanent brain damage—only time will tell. Tell me, do you honestly think it was all worth it? Listen to me, Hannah,' she went on when Hannah sat in silence, her face turned away. 'I don't make rules unnecessarily. They are there because I love you and I don't want any harm to come to you. I want you to have a good and happy life, I want you to have a good job that you enjoy and I don't want you to do anything that you'll live to regret.'

Hannah lifted her head and looked at Olivia. 'Like you did, you mean?' she said.

Olivia felt the colour flood her face. 'What do you mean?'

'Well, let's face it, if you hadn't been foolish, got

yourself pregnant and had me, I imagine your life would have been very different.'

Instinctively Olivia raised her arm and would probably have slapped her daughter if Brad's voice from the doorway hadn't interrupted her.

'Hello. Anybody about? Afraid I'm on the scrounge. I seem to have run out of milk…'

There was a short, tense silence in the kitchen as Olivia struggled for self-control. With a muttered acknowledgement Hannah got up from her chair and, crossing to the fridge, yanked open the door, took out a carton of milk, thrust it into Brad's hands then stalked out of the room.

'I'm sorry,' he said quietly when he and Olivia were alone. 'Looks like I interrupted something there.'

'I'm glad you did.' Her knees trembling, Olivia sank down onto a chair. 'I was about to do something I would have regretted.'

'Want to talk about it?' he asked.

'I told her I didn't want her to make a mess of her life and she flung back in my face what had happened to me.'

'I thought it might have been something like that,' said Brad. 'Really, you know, Olivia, it was inevitable something like this would happen sooner or later.'

'You think so?' she replied wryly. 'I'd hoped she'd been given such a happy childhood the issue wouldn't arise.'

'There's probably no question about whether her childhood was happy or not. This matter wouldn't have arisen until there was a boy on the scene.' He paused. 'Did she tell you about him?'

Olivia nodded. 'Yes, it was Damon. She said she

met him at the youth club, that she'd been out with him a few times and that Charlotte had been out with his friend. She admitted that when she was out with him she'd told me she was at Charlotte's.'

'And the Blakes obviously thought Charlotte was here.'

'Exactly. She said that if she'd told me I wouldn't have let her go.'

'And would you?' Brad raised his eyebrows.

'I don't know. I really don't. But at least we could have discussed it. And if she'd said she had a boyfriend I would have wanted her to bring him here so that I could meet him. I guess she knew I would disapprove because he's a fair bit older than her...' She trailed off helplessly.

'What about the drugs? Was he responsible for those?'

'Hannah says not. She said that was another lad who used to hang about the youth club.'

'So how did they get out to that barn last night? Does Damon have a car?'

Olivia stared at him. 'Do you know, I forgot all about that. I forgot to ask her. Probably he has, which I guess in Hannah's eyes would have been further cause for my disapproval. I shall have to ask her.'

'I can't imagine the matter is closed yet,' said Brad drily.

'Too right it isn't,' Olivia retorted sharply. She fell silent, gazing out of the window at the little paved courtyard at the back of the house. It made a welcome change to see some sunshine after all the recent rain. If only she could appreciate it, instead of having to battle with all this emotional turmoil.

'Have you talked to Hannah very much about her

father?' Brad moved to Olivia's side and she turned
away from the window to look at him.

'We have talked, yes,' she replied. 'Although...'
she hesitated '...I've never actually told her very
much. She knows a certain amount but not all the
details.'

'Maybe it would help if you were to tell her more,'
he suggested slowly. 'It could be that now is the right
time.'

'Yes...maybe.' Olivia sighed. 'I've never told her
he was a fairground worker,' she admitted at last.
'She thinks he was simply working in Malsonbury
then moved on.'

'Does she know that he never knew of her exis-
tence?' he said softly.

Olivia shook her head. 'No, I think she's under the
impression that he just didn't want to know...which,
of course, would have been the case had he been
told,' she added bitterly.

'You don't know that, Olivia,' said Brad.

'What do you mean?' she looked up sharply.

'Well, didn't you tell me that when you saw him
a couple of years later he had a pregnant woman and
a small child with him?'

'Yes, but—'

'He was obviously taking responsibility for them
so there's every reason to believe he may well have
done the same had he known about Hannah.' Brad
paused and in the ensuing silence all that could be
heard was the song of a blackbird outside the window
as it revelled in the unexpected sunshine. 'But I
think,' he went on after a moment, 'it could be very
important for Hannah to know that her father didn't

know about her and therefore didn't actually reject her.'

'But whatever will she think of me for not telling him? I know now how wrong that was, but at the time—'

'You had little choice in the matter. You needed your parents' help…'

'And they'd forbidden me to contact him. I also think Hannah has the idea that I regret what happened, that it has somehow ruined my life.'

'I think you have to tell Hannah that it hasn't. And you know something, Olivia?' Puting his hand beneath her chin, he tilted her face, compelling her to look at him. 'When you tell Hannah these things I think you'll find that the two of you will have a deeper level of understanding than ever before.'

'You could be right,' she replied with a sigh, allowing her gaze to meet his and wishing she could simply drown in his eyes and forget all her troubles.

'Tell me something,' he said, lifting his hand and gently running one finger from her temple down the side of her face and around her cheek before delicately outlining the shape of her mouth. 'Why were you so frosty towards me when we first met?'

'Frosty?' she said—casually, she hoped. 'Was I?'

'Yes, you were. Very frosty. I think if you'd had your way I would have been sent packing straight back to Scotland. I just wondered why.'

She remained silent, battling with her thoughts. As he bent his head and his mouth grew closer to hers she whispered, 'You look like him, Brad.'

'Danny?' he asked softly.

'Yes.'

'Ah.' That was all he said but there was a wealth of understanding in that single syllable.

# CHAPTER ELEVEN

IT HAD been a strange week in many ways. Olivia, sitting at her desk at the end of the last surgery on Friday afternoon, leaned back in her chair and stretched. In the aftermath of the Saturday night barn affair her relationship with Brad had strengthened, but her relationship with Hannah seemed to lurch from the unpredictable to the downright precarious.

Charlotte had continued to improve and had been discharged from hospital into her mother's care in the middle of the week. The police had brought charges, ranging from possession of drugs to supplying them, against several of the young people at the rave. Charges had also been brought against the owner of the barn for failing to provide adequate facilities and for allowing alcohol to be sold to under-age children.

Olivia had been unable to have the conversation with Hannah regarding her father which Brad had suggested. 'I have to address this issue of the rave first,' she'd told him when he'd asked. 'Maybe later when all this calms down, but not yet.'

She'd been to see Charlotte at home and afterwards she'd spoken to Frances in private. 'She's well on the mend,' she said. 'I don't think we need fear any further repercussions.'

'You don't know what a relief that is. Thank you, Olivia,' Frances replied. 'Are you going to discipline Hannah over this?'

'With the exception of the Hallowe'en party this

weekend which we'd already said we'd attend, I've grounded her for a month from going to the youth club or out with her friends,' Olivia replied.

'We've done similar,' Frances admitted, 'although Charlotte won't be going to the Hallowe'en party either. I thought it better that she should rest for the time being. But Geoffrey and I have agreed that her grounding should start from when she has recovered. We've told her the only exception to it will be when the orchestra re-forms. It may seem harsh but we're agreed that she has to learn that that sort of behaviour is totally unacceptable.'

'My sentiments entirely,' Olivia replied. Looking at Frances, she added, 'Our girls are growing up, though, Frances. We have to accept that.'

'Yes, I know.' Frances sighed. 'Maybe when this is over we all need to talk and set new boundaries. On the other hand, if we can only get them interested in their music again…' She trailed off wistfully but Olivia wholeheartedly agreed with her.

Hannah was sulky but strangely resigned to the grounding, and when Olivia mentioned the Hallowe'en party she said, 'If it's all the same to you, I don't think I'll go.'

'Oh, yes, you will,' Olivia was quick to reply. 'For one thing Alison is expecting you, and for another I'm not leaving you here on your own.'

'I suppose you don't trust me.' Hannah's eyes flashed.

'I used to trust you, Hannah. You destroyed that trust. You have to build it up again now.'

Yes, it had been a strange week. Even at the centre things hadn't been straightforward, Scott had continued to be depressed after his break-up with his girlfriend, and David had gone around as if he'd had all the cares of the world upon his shoulders when word had come that James Wilson had decided to return to his duties on a part-time basis only, following his illness.

A light tap at her door broke into Olivia's reflections, and as she looked up Fiona put her head round the door.

'Sorry about this, Olivia, but could you see just one more?'

'Is there no one else available? I was hoping to get away early tonight. We're going away for the weekend.'

Fiona shook her head. 'Sorry, no. David has gone home, Scott has also just left and Brad is out on an emergency.'

'Very well.' Olivia sighed. 'Who is it?'

'It's Tracy Hodges. She has her daughter Leanne's baby with her but I get the impression she just wants to talk to someone.'

'OK. Send her in.'

'Thanks, Olivia.' Fiona paused in the doorway. 'Going anywhere nice?'

'To a friend—she lives near Bath. They're having a Hallowe'en party.'

'Sounds like fun, but have you heard the weather forecast?'

'No. What is it? Tell me the worst.'

'Rain, rain and more rain.' Fiona pulled a face. 'Is Hannah going with you?'

When Olivia nodded Fiona added, 'Just the two of you?'

'Er, no.' Olivia hesitated, knowing how what she

was about to say would be misinterpreted by the reception staff. 'Brad is coming with us, actually.'

'Really?' Fiona raised her eyebrows and there was no mistaking the gleam in her eye.

'Well, he met my friend Alison recently when she came to see me, and she invited him as well…'

'You don't have to explain, Olivia.'

'No, well…' She trailed off, but when Fiona would have disappeared she called her back. 'I'd be obliged if you wouldn't mention it to the girls,' she said. 'You know how they go on…'

'My lips are sealed,' said Fiona with a wink.

Tracy looked tired and drawn when she appeared in the doorway a moment later. She carried the baby in a portable car seat.

'Come in, Tracy, and sit down,' said Olivia. When the woman was seated, perching nervously on the edge of a chair, she said, 'How can I help you. Is it for the baby?'

'No, not really. She's fine.' Tracy's gaze flickered to the baby. 'I had to bring her with me because Leanne is having her hair cut.'

'Did Leanne decide on a name? Sasha—wasn't it that she liked?'

'She changed her mind again in the end and called her Skye—because of her blue eyes, she said.' Tracy hesitated. 'Actually, it's about Leanne that I'm here.'

'Is she not well?' asked Olivia.

'No, it's not that. She's fine. In fact, she's talking about going back to school already. No, it's about what happens next, Dr Chandler.'

'What do you mean, what happens next?'

'Well…' Tracy fidgeted on her chair. 'She says she's going to keep on seeing Craig…'

'The baby's father?'

Tracy nodded. 'Yes. Oh, I understand that he wants to see Skye and I'm glad that he does but, well, I'm a bit worried. What if the same thing happens again?'

'You mean if Leanne gets pregnant again?' asked Olivia.

'Yes.' Tracy nodded, her expression anxious.

'Have you discussed this with Leanne?'

'Well, sort of, and I get the impression that she thinks she'll just go on the Pill. Her sister Kylie is on the Pill, you see.'

'And would it bother you if Leanne went on the Pill?'

'Well, yes, I think it would.' Tracy glanced at the sleeping baby again. 'Oh, don't get me wrong,' she added hastily. 'I don't want her to have another one, but she is only just fifteen... What I'm saying is...she shouldn't...should she?'

'No, Tracy. You're quite right. Leanne is under-age and so, from what I gather, is her boyfriend. By having sex, they're breaking the law.'

'But what do I say to her?' For a fleeting moment a look of utter despair crossed Tracy's face. 'If I tell her she mustn't do it, and that she shouldn't go on the Pill, she may end up having another one. She is, after all, not a little girl now, she's a mother... It's different for Kylie, she's seventeen, but Leanne, well...' She gave a helpless little shrug. 'Honestly, Dr Chandler, I'm at my wits' end. I don't know what to do.'

'It's not easy, is it, bringing up teenagers in today's world?' Olivia gave her a sympathetic smile.

Tracy shook her head. 'I bet you don't have these problems with your daughter, Doctor.'

Outwardly, with a cool smile, Olivia retained her composure. 'Tell Leanne to come and see me, will you? I'll talk to her. I'm not saying I can work any miracles but I can maybe establish what her intentions are so that the necessary measures can be taken.' She stopped and looked keenly at Tracy. 'And what about you?' she said.

'Me?' said Tracy in surprise. 'Oh, I'm all right.'

'You have a lot on your plate and there'll be even more presumably when Leanne goes back to school. You're looking very pale, Tracy—and tired.'

'Well, I do get tired, but I suppose that's understandable. I don't seem to stop these days. There's something to do all the time.'

'Are your periods all right?' asked Olivia as she checked Tracy's history and medication chart on her computer screen.

'Well, they're regular if that's what you mean.'

'Heavier than usual?'

Tracy paused to consider. 'Yes, I suppose they are now you come to mention it.'

Olivia leaned forward and gently eased down one of Tracy's lower eyelids. 'You may be a bit anaemic,' she said. 'Make an appointment on your way out with the nurse for a blood test.'

'What would it mean if I was?' asked Tracy in alarm. 'I couldn't go into hospital—not now.'

'Don't worry, Tracy, probably all it will mean is that you need a course of iron tablets, which I can prescribe for you.'

When Tracy had gone Olivia sat for a while, reflecting on their conversation. Privately her heart ached for this woman who, like so many other parents, had inadvertently become a victim of the times and was bewildered as to why it should have happened.

'Penny for them?'

She looked up sharply to find Brad standing in the doorway, watching her. Her heart gave the funny little lurch it always did whenever she unexpectedly caught sight of him. 'Sorry?' she said.

'Your thoughts. You were miles away.'

'Was I? Yes, I suppose I was. I was thinking about how hard it is to be the parent of teenagers in today's society. I've just seen Tracy Hodges—remember Tracy—Leanne's and Kylie's mum?'

'Oh, yes. How is she?'

'Struggling.'

'I can imagine. Just as I would think her troubles are ongoing rather than ones that could have a simple solution.'

Olivia nodded and they were silent for a moment. Brad had come right into her room, pushing the door shut behind him. Now he was perched on the front of her desk and was toying with a tray containing pens, pencils and paperclips.

'You were looking for me?'

'Yes, I've just had a letter from the hospital concerning Stephen Trowbridge. I thought you might be interested.'

'Oh, yes, I am. How is he?'

'Much better apparently. He responded well after his transfusion and if he continues to improve he'll be discharged at the weekend.'

'Well, that's a relief.'

'He still has a long way to go with his chemotherapy programme but, according to his consultant, he can't wait to get back to his chess sessions at the hospice with old Samuel.'

'Good for Stephen. Let's hope he's an example to his friends.' With a sigh Olivia stood up. 'Have you finished, Brad?'

'Yes, have you?'

She nodded. 'Tracy was the last. I don't know about you but I'm for home.'

'Me, too.' As she picked up her case and came round the desk he stood up and opened the door for her.

Taking her trench coat from the back of the door, she attempted to pass him, but because of the coat and the case she was carrying the space was limited and she was forced to press closely against him. He didn't move immediately and questioningly she allowed her eyes to meet his. There was a quizzical expression in his own eyes as his gaze roamed over her face, finally coming to rest on her mouth.

'What?' she said.

'I've been thinking,' he said softly.

'Yes?'

'If the reason for your coolness towards me when I first came here was because I look like Danny, I can only assume that fact must have bothered you in some way.' He paused and his gaze moved to her eyes then lingeringly back to her mouth.

'Oh, it did,' she said softly. 'You know it did.'

'And now?' he said.

'You still bother me,' she whispered, 'but not because you look like Danny.'

'I'm glad to hear it,' he said with a soft chuckle.

It was still raining the following day when Olivia, Brad and Hannah set out for Bath. Because of storm and flood warnings it was decided they'd take Brad's Range Rover rather than Olivia's smaller car.

'It even has an inflatable dinghy in the boot,' he joked as they drew out of the square, 'so if we get marooned anywhere by the floods I'll be able to row you both to safety.'

'This vehicle of yours is quite amazing.' Olivia laughed as she fastened her seat belt. 'Not only is it equipped as a mobile paramedic unit, it's also a complete rescue service.'

'Why is it like that?' Hannah leaned forward between the front seats.

'It was essential in my Pitlochry practice,' Brad explained. 'There was no knowing what to expect on a call-out. Some of our patients lived many miles away in far-flung homesteads and sheep farms, and the going was sometimes over very rough terrain and in all kinds of weather. I remember one winter, being called out to a farmer's wife who'd had a suspected heart attack. There had been blizzards for three days and the roads were barely passable. There was no way an ambulance was going to get up there so it was all down to us.'

'Us?' Olivia turned her head to look at him.

'Yes, I took a nurse with me in case we had to bring the patient back to the hospital in Pitlochry...' He stopped and Olivia saw that the shadowed look was back on his face.

'And did you?' demanded Hannah.

'Did we what?' The look had gone, having vanished as quickly as it had arrived.

'Get to the patient in time and bring her back?'

'Oh, yes. But it was touch and go, I can tell you.

The patient was very weak but thanks to the equipment I carry on board—the defibrillator and the oxygen—and the fact that this vehicle is a four-wheel-drive, we made it back. The patient went into Intensive Care and, as far as I know, she's still alive and healthy and living on her farm.'

'Did you ever do any mountain rescue?' Olivia really wanted to ask about the nurse who had accompanied him on that trip and why he'd looked that way when he'd mentioned her. Had she been the reason he was leaving Scotland? Had she been the one who'd hurt him so much? Instead, she found herself asking about mountain rescue because for some reason she still lacked the courage to broach that particular subject. It was almost as if she couldn't bear the answers he might give about the woman who had obviously meant everything to him.

'Oh, yes, quite often,' he replied in answer to her question. 'We were right on the edge of the Grampians and the Trossachs so there was a great deal of mountain-climbing in the area. Walkers, too, would set out with insufficient equipment and if the weather turned bad they'd find themselves trapped. The rescue teams would be called and would very often require the assistance of a doctor.'

'Do you miss all that?' Hannah was obviously fascinated by what he was saying. 'It sounds so exciting.'

'I imagine there'll be similar situations in the region I'm going to in Canada.'

They fell silent after that, as if mention of Canada and his departure from their lives had put a damper on the conversation.

As they neared the area where Alison and Paul

lived there was much evidence of recent flooding. Fields were under water for miles around and it became obvious that the river, in full spate, had burst its banks. The village of Browton was situated on an incline a few miles south of the motorway and when they arrived, although it was still raining heavily, they were relieved to find the roads in and around the village weren't flooded.

The Vincents lived in a seventeenth-century cottage in a lane that ran alongside the Norman church. Their neighbours on one side were the vicar and his wife and on the other a family who had recently converted a barn into living accommodation.

'What a fabulous spot.' Brad pulled up his collar as he opened his door.

'It's even better in the sunshine.' Olivia gave a wry smile.

Alison and Paul were at the door to greet them, together with Harry, their three-year-old son, who eyed the newcomers suspiciously.

'We were hoping you'd bring some better weather with you.' Alison opened her arms to embrace Olivia.

'What were the roads like?' asked Paul, after shaking hands with Brad.

'The roads weren't too bad, but the fields were under water.'

'We're hoping everyone will be able to get here for the party.' Alison hugged Hannah. 'As it is, there was some doubt whether Paul's sister, June, would be able to come. Her baby is due literally at any minute. Her husband, Ian, was doubtful about them coming but I told him not to worry because we'd have no less than two doctors in attendance. I say…' She stopped and held Hannah at arm's length. 'You *did* bring your clarinet, didn't you?'

'Of course…' Hannah grinned and Alison turned swiftly to Brad.

'And you your saxophone?'

He smiled and nodded.

'Oh, good. I've told absolutely everyone how good you both are.'

Alison took them to their rooms while Paul went off to the kitchen to brew a pot of tea. Hannah and Olivia were to share one of the bedrooms under the eaves while Brad was down the corridor.

'So how's it going, then?' It was a little later and Alison had come back upstairs to Olivia's room. Hannah had gone downstairs to play with Harry while Brad could be heard talking to Paul in the kitchen.

'How's what going?' Olivia looked up from unpacking her overnight bag.

'Well, you and Brad, of course. What did you think I meant?' Alison sat on the side of the bed. It was just like old times when the two girls had got together in their rooms after school and shared their secrets.

'I thought you might have meant your mum,' Olivia replied lightly, but the look she threw Alison from beneath her lashes suggested otherwise.

'I know that Mum is doing very well and I'm deeply grateful to you for that, but that wasn't what I was meaning. I'm dying to know what's happening between you and Brad. Go on, do tell.'

'I'm not sure that anything is exactly happening.' Olivia straightened up, a neat little pile of silk lingerie in her arms.

'Oh, go on. You can't fool me. You've only got to see the way he looks at you. While you…'

'Me? What about me?' Olivia's eyes widened.

'I haven't seen you like this for years—there's this aura about you. You're glowing, Livvy! And it's wonderful!'

'It's a pity it can't last, then, isn't it?'

Alison stared at her for a moment. 'Oh, you mean the Canada thing?' Her reply was dismissive. 'I told you, he either won't go or you'll go with him.'

'Its not that easy,' Olivia protested. 'For a start I dare say he's signed a contract by now so he'll have to go, and I couldn't just up sticks and leave. I have the practice to consider and there's Hannah—her schooling is at a crucial stage. Besides, who's to say he'd want me to go with him? No, Ali, I'm not letting myself get too involved with him. That way I won't have too many pieces to pick up when it ends.'

Shortly after six o'clock people began arriving for the party. Alison and Paul had decorated the cottage with masks and candles that glowed from within hollowed-out pumpkins. Some of the younger guests came in fancy dress as witches or goblins, vampires or ghosts.

Paul dispensed mulled wine heavily spiced with cinnamon, and while guests enjoyed their drinks and a delicious selection of canapés Alison persuaded Brad and Hannah to provide background music.

The party was beginning to go with a real swing when Alison made her way across to Olivia who was perched on the stairs, sipping her wine and enjoying the music.

'What's up?' Olivia said. 'You look worried.'

'Not really worried. Just a bit concerned, that's all. June and Ian haven't arrived yet.'

'How far have they to come?'

'About twenty miles. They live out towards Midsomer Norton. Paul tried to phone about an hour ago but there was no reply so presumably they'd already left. They should have been here by now.'

'Maybe they called in to see someone on the way.'

'Yes, maybe.' Alison sounded far from convinced. 'We probably wouldn't be concerned if the weather wasn't so atrocious.'

'And if June's baby wasn't imminent.'

'Yes. Quite.' Alison moved away and Brad, who had stopped playing, came and sat beside Olivia. Hannah, who was also taking a rest, had been drawn into a group of young people and was in conversation with a boy dressed as a vampire.

'She's really very promising, you know,' said Brad, looking at Hannah. 'She needs practice, that's all.'

'Rejoining the orchestra will be good for her.' Olivia nodded. 'And you going with her will be an added incentive.'

'I'm quite looking forward to it,' he replied with a laugh. 'It's years since I played in an orchestra.'

As they sat, chatting easily to each other, totally relaxed in each other's company, the sound of Hannah's laughter floated across the room towards them.

'She sounds happy with her vampire,' observed Brad.

'At least he's her age, vampire or not.' Olivia gave a wry smile.

'I don't think you'll have too much more trouble with her. Last weekend really knocked the wind out of her sails and I think it came home to her that she nearly lost Charlotte.'

'I only hope you're right...' Olivia trailed off as,

through the gathering throng, she caught a glimpse of Paul, a worried expression on his face as he talked to Alison.

'I think there's something wrong,' she said.

'What do you mean?' Brad looked up sharply.

'Alison told me a while ago that Paul's sister and her husband haven't arrived yet. They've tried ringing them and there's no reply at their home.'

'This is the mum-to-be?' Brad turned to look at Alison and Paul who were deep in conversation.

'Yes... I think I'll go and see what's happening.' Olivia scrambled to her feet.

'I'll come with you.'

Alison turned as they approached and a look of relief passed swiftly across her face, as if simply by talking to them matters would be put right.

'No sign of them?' asked Brad.

Paul shook his head. 'No. They aren't at home and they've had more than ample time to get here. I've even phoned the obstetric unit to see if June has been admitted but she hasn't. I'm really worried that something may have happened...what with this weather and everything...'

'Would you like me to drive out in the direction they would have taken and see if I can see them?' asked Brad.

'That's very kind of you,' said Paul, 'but really I should go...'

'What car do you have?' asked Brad.

'A Mondeo...'

'No. I'll go. The Range Rover will hold the road better if there's a lot of water to go through and, besides, you have your guests...'

'What if they've had an accident?'

'I have a mobile phone. I can contact the emergency services if necessary.'

'Suppose June is in trouble,' said Alison fearfully.

'Then she'll be glad of a doctor,' Brad replied calmly.

'Two doctors would be even better—I'll come with you.' Olivia set down her glass on a small coffee-table.

'Good idea.' Brad smiled. 'Obstetrics never was my strong point.'

# CHAPTER TWELVE

IN MANY places where the river had burst its banks
the water had seeped from the fields and was lying
across the road, and where the road dipped the water
was deep. The Range Rover held the road well and,
mercifully, for a while at least, the rain had eased and
dark clouds scudded across a watery-looking moon.

If their mission hadn't been one of such anxiety
Olivia might have found the situation incredibly romantic, sitting there beside Brad in the moonlight
with the flood waters all around them as, in an un-
canny silence, they traversed the deserted countryside.

'What do you think has happened to them?' asked
Olivia as she gazed around at the awesome and unfamiliar landscape.

'I think they could well have broken down—you
know, water in the engine or something like that.'
Brad paused. 'On the other hand, maybe when they
realised just how bad the conditions were they turned
back.'

In the meagre light from the moon tall grasses,
reeds and hedges could be seen above the water, and
here and there a solitary tree. Once they passed a
farmhouse, dark and silent, the water lapping around
its walls. A breeze had sprung up since the rain had
stopped, ruffling the surface of the flood water and
giving it a desolate, slightly sinister appearance.

Olivia shivered, suddenly incredibly grateful for

the protection of the vehicle in which they were travelling.

'How far have we come?' She tried to peer farther into the distance beyond the beam of the headlights but it hurt her eyes and she gave up the attempt. 'It's hard to tell, travelling so slowly.'

'About seven miles.' Brad glanced at the milometer. 'It just seems much farther.'

They fell silent again and had travelled another couple of miles or so when Olivia suddenly leaned forward. 'Look,' she said urgently, 'there's something there just ahead under those trees. What is it?'

Brad slowed down and looked towards where Olivia was pointing. A dark shape could be seen protruding from the flood water that swirled around it.

'It's a car!' she cried. 'It must be them!'

'The ground rises ahead,' Brad replied. 'I'll drive up there and stop where it's dry.'

Moments later they had left the Range Rover and were hurrying back down the hill towards the other car. Both of them carried torches and Brad had a staff to test the depth of the water. Olivia was grateful for the gumboots Alison and Paul had insisted they wore. As they drew closer, with the water lapping around their ankles, they could see that the car must have skidded right across the road and appeared to have lurched into a water-filled storm trench. It was lodged against the trunk of a tree, tilted almost on its side at a crazy angle. There was no sound from within and, fearful of what they might find, Olivia watched as Brad flashed his torch down into the interior of the car.

In the light from the torch they caught sight of a woman's white face in the passenger seat.

With a muttered exclamation Brad leaned forward and attempted to wrench open the door. 'It's locked,' he muttered. He knocked on the window with his knuckles. 'Open the door,' he shouted.

The woman's face appeared again. She looked terrified.

'Let her see you.' Brad turned briefly to Olivia. 'She's frightened. It may help if she sees another woman.'

Olivia bent down and peered into the car. 'It's all right,' she shouted. 'June, we've come to help you.'

There was another moment of silence then they heard the woman scrabbling at the door lock. Brad tried the handle again and this time he was able to pull the door open. Because of the angle of the car, he had to hold tightly to the door to prevent it from slamming shut again.

Now that she could see the interior, Olivia could quite clearly make out that beside the woman was the figure of a man, slumped partly against the dashboard and partly against the far door. He appeared to be covered in blood and the woman was leaning across him, holding a wad of material to his forehead in an attempt to staunch the flow.

'He's hurt…' she gasped over her shoulder. 'He hit his head.'

'It's all right, June,' said Brad. 'We've come to help you. We're friends of Paul and Alison and we're also doctors.'

'Oh, thank goodness. Thank goodness.' The woman began to sob.

'Are you all right, June?' asked Olivia urgently.

'No… I've got pains. I think…I think the baby's coming…'

'Right.' Brad took immediate control. 'We need to get you out of there and into the Range Rover.' He half turned to Olivia. 'We need to move fast before the car fills up with water.'

'But…Ian…my husband…' quavered the woman.

'We'll see to him as well—don't worry.' Brad turned to Olivia again. 'I'm going to try to ease her out of the car. Will you hold the torch?'

Somehow, between them, they managed to help June to turn until she was sitting on the side edge of her seat.

'How deep is the water?' she gasped.

'It's all right,' Olivia reassured her. 'It's only ankle-deep just here. It's only down there in the ditch that it's much deeper. Now, if I help you, do you think you could manage to walk up there to the Range Rover?' She pointed to the top of the hill where Brad's vehicle could quite clearly be seen in the moonlight.

'I'll try…'

'How often are your pains coming?'

'Very often. About every two minutes, I think…' Clutching her swollen abdomen, June struggled to her feet and Brad scrambled forward and down into the car.

'Is your husband unconscious?' asked Olivia.

'No.' June shook her head. 'But he doesn't really seem to be with it… And there's so much blood… I didn't know what to do—' She gave a sudden cry as a contraction gripped her. 'I think I want to push,' she groaned.

Olivia put her arm around her and, supporting her as best she could, they began very slowly to walk up the hill.

By the time Olivia had pulled down the seats in the back of Brad's vehicle to form a couch and had settled June as comfortably as she could, Brad had got back with Ian whom he eased into the front passenger seat, before attending to his injury.

Olivia joined him a few moments later, after examining June, and they stood together outside the Range Rover. 'Are you going to phone for an ambulance?' she asked.

'How far is June into labour?' He glanced into the back of the vehicle.

'Contractions are coming regularly and very close together, and her cervix is well dilated.'

'In that case, I think it's probably best if we just press on to the hospital. There's no point in calling an ambulance. In these conditions it would take far too long for them to get here.'

'What about her husband? How is he?'

'He has a nasty gash above his right eyebrow,' Brad replied, 'and I think he's suffering from a certain amount of concussion. He's very disorientated but the bleeding has eased and I've put temporary steri-strips over his cut.'

'All right. I'll travel in the back with June while you drive. Give me your mobile phone and I'll phone the hospital to warn them and Alison and Paul to set their minds at ease.'

While Brad started up the engine and drew away, turning round in the first appropriate place for the drive back, Olivia made the two phone calls. She spoke to Alison first to inform her what was happening.

'But June—how is she?' Alison asked anxiously

after Olivia had told her that Ian had been injured but not seriously.

'June is in labour,' Olivia replied.

'What?'

'Yes, we're taking her straight to the hospital. Can you give me the number, please?'

'Oh, yes. Yes, of course.' There was a few moments' delay while Alison found the number.

'Thanks, Ali.' Olivia jotted the number on the back of her wrist. 'We'll be back with you as soon as we can.'

Brad drove on carefully. In some places there was little standing water on the road, in others it was quite deep. Ian remained very quiet and subdued in the front seat, but in the rear of the vehicle June grew more and more restless.

Olivia crouched over her in the confined space and for the umpteenth time listened for the baby's heartbeat through Brad's stethoscope.

'Oh,' gasped June as she gripped Olivia's hand. 'There's another pain coming…and I want to push… I've got to push…'

'Brad.' Olivia leaned forward and touched him on the shoulder. 'I'm sorry, but you'll have to stop again. This baby simply isn't going to wait. I need some more light and I need for us to be still.'

'All right. I'll pull in over there.' He peered ahead. 'Hopefully, there isn't too much water just there, otherwise we might not get going again.'

Once he'd stopped Brad came round to the rear of the vehicle where he crawled in beside Olivia and held both torches to give her the maximum amount of light.

'There are some clean towels in that case.' He

pointed to a container under the seat. 'And there are blankets over there.'

The conditions were both cramped and awkward and the facilities limited, but Olivia remained calm as she gave June the encouragement she needed. 'Come on,' she said as she felt a contraction peak. 'Nice big push.'

The contractions came fast after that, with June gasping with the pain before pushing and bearing down strongly then panting in short, sharp gasps as Olivia instructed her to do.

'I can see the baby's head,' said Olivia at last. 'Come on, June, one more big push... Now...'

Brad held the torches steady as the baby's head was delivered. Olivia instructed June in her breathing to slow things down a little, holding the tiny head with its wet, matted crown of black hair in her hands until, with another huge contraction, June pushed once more. Olivia turned the baby's shoulders just seconds before the rest of its body was expelled.

Quickly she cleared the baby's airways. As its first thin wail pierced the stillness of the night Ian seemed to come out of his stupor and turned his head.

'You have a daughter,' said Olivia, holding the baby so that the new mother could see her. Moments later another contraction expelled the afterbirth. Keeping everything intact, not wanting to risk infection by cutting the umbilical cord, Olivia wrapped baby, cord and afterbirth first in the clean towels and then in a tartan blanket. She gave the precious bundle to a tired but euphoric June, before covering her with another blanket.

'Right, Dr Bradley.' She turned to Brad. 'Hospital now, as fast as you can.'

Just for a moment his eyes met hers. 'Well done, Dr Chandler,' he said softly, before switching off the torches. 'Well done.'

'I doubt if we'll ever see another Hallowe'en like this one.'

It was much later and Brad and Olivia were driving back to Alison and Paul's home. They had arrived safely at the hospital where they had taken June and the baby to the obstetric unit and Ian to Accident and Emergency to have his wound stitched, treatment for shock and for X-rays for his suspected concussion. He had seemed unaware that June had given birth to their daughter in spite of that brief moment when he'd appeared to have heard the baby's first cry.

'He's going to have a shock when he's finally with it again,' Brad had said as they'd left A and E. In the foyer they'd met Paul who'd driven to the hospital after receiving Olivia's message and who'd been waiting anxiously there ever since. He'd been amazed to be told he was already an uncle and that mother and baby were doing well. 'I think I'll stay here for a while,' he'd told them. 'I want to make sure that Ian is all right, and maybe later they'll let me see June and my new niece.'

Olivia turned, looked at Brad's profile and smiled at his words. 'You're right,' she said. 'You don't somehow associate Hallowe'en with newborn babies—or floods, come to that.'

'Tonight has been quite special,' he said, and there was a little catch in his voice. 'I don't think I shall ever forget it. I've delivered babies before, just as I'm sure you have, but this was different... You and I working together... I can't explain it...'

'You don't have to,' she said softly. 'I know what you mean. It was special for me, too.'

Without a word he drew to the side of the road. Switching off the engine, he turned to her, leaned forward and drew her into his arms.

She wanted him to kiss her—longed for it, in fact—but instead she pulled away. In the darkness she sensed his surprise.

'Olivia?' he said. 'What is it? What's wrong?'

'I can't,' she said simply.

'Why?'

'Because if I do I won't be able to bear it when you go away.'

There was a long silence between them before Brad spoke. 'What would you say,' he said slowly, 'if I were to tell you that I've decided not to go to Canada after all?'

For one incredible moment her heart leapt crazily as unimaginable possibilities crowded into her mind, then reality reasserted itself and she turned her face towards him. 'But you have to go. You have a job to go to.'

'I haven't signed the final contract yet.'

'But you want to go, Brad. You need to go—to get away—to start afresh. Wasn't that what you said?'

'Yes. That's true. That's exactly what I said and, yes, there was a situation at home in Scotland that I felt I needed to distance myself from.'

Here it comes, she thought. What she'd been dreading to hear. The all-consuming affair with the woman who'd meant everything to him but who'd hurt him so much that he felt he couldn't bear to see her again.

'I think, Olivia, I need to tell you about it—that is, if you're prepared to listen.'

'Of course.' Her reply was firm, sympathetic even, but inside her emotions were in turmoil. Mentally she braced herself as he began to speak.

'There was a girl,' he said. 'Her name was Teresa. She was the daughter of my father's partner and we grew up together. There was no secret made of the fact in our families that they all hoped we would marry. I thought I was in love with Teresa, and at one time it seemed there would be nothing easier than for us to marry, have a family and for me to become a partner in the practice our fathers had set up. I went away to university and medical school but when I became a houseman things began to change. My world opened up and I began to question my feelings for Teresa.'

'Did she still feel the same way about you?'

'Yes, she did. That's what made things very difficult. I knew I should tell her that my feelings had changed but somehow I never seemed to find the right time. She'd trained as a nurse and by the time I returned to Pitlochry as a partner she, too, was working in the practice. At that time everyone seemed to be pressurising us to get married and I knew the time was fast approaching when I would have to do something.'

'So what happened?' Olivia frowned in the darkness. This was turning out to be a vastly different story from the one she'd imagined.

'Teresa fell ill. She developed a variety of worrying symptoms which didn't seem to lead to any clear-cut diagnosis. She had dozens of tests until at last one of them revealed she was suffering from acute leukaemia. Unfortunately, by the time the diagnosis was made it had progressed too far. Teresa died in my arms six months later. I never told her of my change of feelings and I'm glad now that I didn't. She died believing that had she lived we would have been married...'

'Oh, Brad...I'm so sorry,' Olivia whispered as his voice faltered. So much now had been explained, especially that dark, shadowed expression she'd glimpsed in his eyes on several occasions.

'I had to get away,' he said. 'I may have realised that Teresa wasn't the woman I should be marrying, but we'd grown up as brother and sister and I felt as if I'd lost my best friend.' He stopped and the only sound to be heard was the distant whistle of a train as it sped through some small deserted town.

'I had this instinct all along,' he went on after a while, 'that the feeling I had for Teresa wasn't the right sort of feeling I should have if I was contemplating marrying her, and now, since coming here and meeting you, I know I was right.'

'Brad...'

'No, let me finish, please. From the moment I met you, Olivia, I knew what I felt was different. All I wanted was to be where you were. Even when you tried to freeze me out I didn't care. I very soon knew that this was love and I knew that I had been right not to marry Teresa because I had never felt this way about her.'

'And there was me keeping you at arm's length because you looked like Danny. You brought back all the old feelings and memories. It was crazy. I thought that because you looked like him you would *be* like him... And later, even when I was beginning to realise you were nothing like Danny at all, I began to think you were running away from some situation that probably involved another woman.'

'Well, I guess you were right there.'

'Yes, but the truth was as far removed as it could have been from what I had thought. And then, as if all that wasn't enough, when I did begin to admit to myself that I felt something for you, I had to try and suppress it because I couldn't bear the thought that you were going away shortly and would probably be out of my life for ever.'

'I can't go away, Olivia. I know that now. I couldn't bear to be separated from you.'

'But what will you do?' Even as the possibility entered her mind he voiced it.

'I was wondering if the practice would consider me as a partner?' he said hesitantly. 'I know David was saying they would have to look for another partner as James is only able to work on a part-time basis in the future. What do you think?'

'What do I think? Oh, Brad, that would be perfect…just perfect. The others have already said it's a pity you're going to Canada as you'd be so right for the practice.'

'Only for the practice?' he asked softly.

'Oh, no,' she replied happily. 'For me as well.'

This time there was no pulling away when he tried to kiss her. This time she gave herself up quite happily and wound her arms around his neck, knowing that he was here to stay and that there would be no heart-breaking parting. As the desire leapt inside her she knew at last that she had found her soul mate, the man with whom she would spend the rest of her life.

'I love you, Olivia,' he murmured between kisses. 'Stay with me for ever.'

'Oh, yes,' she replied. 'Oh, yes.'


'Mum, I need to tell you something.' Hannah came into Olivia's bedroom and sat down on the edge of the bed. It was the Friday evening of the week following their return from Bath, and Hannah had just returned from school.

'What is it?' Olivia turned swiftly from her dressing-table. There was something in Hannah's tone that caused her a tremor of anxiety.

'Damon was waiting for me at the school gates.'

'What did he want?' asked Olivia. She'd had a long day in surgery and feared a scene with her daughter, but she knew, in view of recent events, she couldn't shirk this.

'He wanted to know if I was still going out with him,' said Hannah.

'And what did you say?'

'I told him that, no, we were finished.'

'Why did you tell him that?' asked Olivia in surprise. She had quite been expecting Hannah to say she wanted to bring Damon home.

'I found out from some of the others that he'd been charged with possessing drugs.'

Olivia caught her breath. 'I thought you said he wasn't into anything like that.'

'I know. I did. That's what I thought. Just shows how wrong you can be, doesn't it?'

Olivia glanced sharply at her daughter and saw her lip tremble and the glistening of tears in her eyes.

'I don't want to be mixed up in any of that,' Hannah said. 'I never did. I know how it ruins people's lives—you've told me that often enough. And now, after what's happened to Charlotte and every-thing... So I told him...'

'Oh, I am sorry, Hannah.' Olivia put out her hand and covered her daughter's where it lay on the bed. 'It hurts, doesn't it, when you've really cared about someone?'

Hannah nodded, dashing away the tears as they trickled down her cheeks. 'Has anything like that ever happened to you?' she asked with a sniff.

'Oh, yes,' said Olivia quietly. 'It has. It happened with your father.'

Hannah looked up sharply, the surprise on her face only too evident as Olivia brought up this little-talked-about subject.

'Would you like me to tell you about him?'

Hannah nodded. 'Yes,' she replied slowly. 'Yes, I think so.'

Olivia took a deep breath. 'I was very young at the time. He was a bit older than me and I thought he was absolutely gorgeous. I fell head over heels in love with him, Hannah. Unfortunately I was very foolish and I allowed myself to become pregnant.'

'What happened?' whispered Hannah. 'Didn't he want me?'

'He never knew about you,' replied Olivia quietly.

Hannah blinked. 'What do you mean—he never even knew you were pregnant?'

Olivia shook her head.

'But why didn't you tell him?' Hannah looked amazed.

'He'd gone by the time I found out. Moved on. I'd written to him before then but he'd never replied to my letters. I was heart-broken at the time because I thought he loved me as much as I loved him. I've since realised I was probably just one of many.' She paused. 'I imagine there was a different girl in every town. He worked in a travelling fairground, Hannah.'

'You mean like a gypsy?' breathed Hannah, who was, no doubt, thinking the whole thing sounded incredibly romantic.

'Yes, just like a gypsy.'

'What did Nanna and Gramps think about that?' Hannah's eyes were like saucers now.

'They weren't pleased,' admitted Olivia. 'I had just completed my A levels at the time and was all set for medical school. When I told them I wanted to keep the baby they persuaded me that the best thing to do was not to get in touch with...with Danny again. They said that they would care for the baby when it was born and that I could continue with my studies.

'And that, Hannah, is exactly what happened. Maybe it was wrong, I don't know. There would be those who would say that Danny had a right to know and there would be others who would say that you have a right to be able to contact your father. All I know is that your grandparents and I did what we felt was right at the time.'

'But didn't you want to see him again? You said you loved him so much...' There was bewilderment in Hannah's eyes now.

'Yes, I did, and I carried on loving him long after you were born, but I think even then I knew that it would never have worked out.'

'And you never saw him again?'

'I saw him once. He didn't see me,' Olivia replied. 'He was with a woman, Hannah, a very pregnant woman who already had one small child not much younger than you.'

'Oh…' Hannah's eyes became round again as she took in this piece of information.

'I think from that moment on I started to get over him.' Olivia paused and looked at Hannah. 'However, if you feel you want to try and find him, I won't stand in your way.'

'I don't know…' Hannah slowly shook her head. 'I used to think I'd like to see my father. I would dream about going to find him…but if he doesn't know about me, it would be a tremendous shock if I suddenly turned up, wouldn't it? And then there's his wife or girlfriend or whatever she was—it would cause all sorts of trouble there, wouldn't it?'

Olivia nodded, struck suddenly by her daughter's unexpected level of maturity. 'Yes,' she agreed, 'I dare say it would.'

'I always thought it would be nice to have a father,' said Hannah. 'But I'm not sure I would want all that sort of hassle…'

'Actually, while we're on that subject there's something else I think you should know,' said Olivia.

Hannah stared at her and there must have been something in her mother's face that told her. 'It's Brad, isn't it?' she cried. When Olivia nodded, Hannah flung her arms around her neck. 'Oh, I knew it! I knew it! Oh, I'm so pleased!'

'Are you? Are you really pleased?' asked Olivia as the breath caught in her throat.

'Yes, yes, I am. I think he's the nicest man I've ever met,' said Hannah. 'For an oldie, that is,' she added with a grin. 'But what about Canada?'

'He's decided not to go to Canada,' Olivia replied. 'He's going to stay here and it's more than likely that he'll become a partner at the practice. Dr Wilson isn't going to be able to resume full-time duties, and to save Dr Skinner from collapsing with stress it's been decided to take on another full-time partner. Brad more than fits the bill.'

'That's really cool. He'll be able to stay with the orchestra now. They all thought he was great when he came with me during the week.' Hannah paused. 'What will happen? Will he live here?'

'We're going to be married, Hannah, and, yes, we will still live here. At least, for the time being.'

'Oh, that's good.' Hannah looked relieved and they were silent for a moment, each reflecting and busy with her own thoughts. It was Olivia who broke the silence. Standing up, she crossed to her wardrobe and opened the door. 'You will get over Damon, you know,' she said.

'Oh, I know,' Hannah replied. There was another silence. 'Actually,' she said, 'I had a letter this morning.'

'Oh?' said Olivia, without turning round. There was nothing unusual in the post coming after she'd left for work.

'Yes,' Hannah went on, 'it was from Luke.'

'Luke?' Olivia turned then and frowned. 'Do I know Luke?'

'Yes.' Hannah laughed. 'Although the last time you saw him he was a vampire.'

'The vampire, you say?' Brad raised a quizzical eyebrow.

'Yes, his name is Luke and apparently he's going to be a doctor, and I quote, "just like me", Hannah told me.'

'Can we take that to mean the modelling phase is over?'

'I guess we can. At least she's talking about A levels again. It seems she and Luke have got some sort of bet over who's going to get the most GSCEs and the highest grades.'

'Did you tell her about us?' asked Brad. He leaned forward and Olivia thought she detected a trace of anxiety in his voice. They were sitting in the conservatory, surrounded by the Sunday papers, with a tray of toast, orange juice and coffee on the table between them.

'I did,' she replied lightly.

'And?' The anxiety was tempered with curiosity now.

Olivia looked up, her gaze meeting his. Her heart gave its usual little flutter at the expression in his eyes. 'She was delighted,' she answered in the same light tone.

'Ah.' His breath caught in his throat.

'Her actual words were that you are the nicest man she has ever met.' She smiled as his colour deepened. 'I do believe you're blushing, Dr Bradley!'

'Well, it's not every day you get an opinion like that from a charming young lady,' he replied.

'She actually went on to say "for an oldie".'

Olivia ducked as he threw a cushion at her across the conservatory then they both returned to their papers.

'You know something?' he said after a while. 'We're just like an old married couple, sitting here over brunch with the Sunday papers.'

Olivia laughed. 'Yes, and even discussing the youth of today.'

'There's only one thing missing,' he went on, and as Olivia looked up she saw that certain look was back in his eyes. 'And I've been thinking, now that Hannah knows about us there's nothing to stop me moving in here now, is there?'

'Dr Bradley!' Olivia adopted her most shocked expression. 'I don't know how you can even think such a thing. What sort of example would we be setting to Hannah if you were to do that before we were married?'

He sighed. 'It was worth a try. But I suppose you're right.'

There was silence for a moment then Olivia said, 'On the other hand, Hannah has gone over to Charlotte's to do some revision. She said she won't be back until this evening...'

'Really?' He stood up and held out his hand. 'That settles it then. Your place or mine?'

'Oh, I think yours,' she said with a chuckle as she rose to her feet and took his hand. 'That way we can be absolutely certain we won't be disturbed.'

# MILLS & BOON®

*Makes any time special*™

*Mills & Boon publish 29 new titles every month. Select from...*

Modern Romance™         Tender Romance™

Sensual Romance™

Medical Romance™  Historical Romance™

MAT2

# 4 FREE

## books and a surprise gift!

We would like to take this opportunity to thank you for reading this Mills & Boon® book by offering you the chance to take FOUR more specially selected titles from the Medical Romance™ series absolutely FREE! We're also making this offer to introduce you to the benefits of the Reader Service™—

- ★ FREE home delivery
- ★ FREE gifts and competitions
- ★ FREE monthly Newsletter
- ★ Exclusive Reader Service discounts
- ★ Books available before they're in the shops

Accepting these FREE books and gift places you under no obligation to buy, you may cancel at any time, even after receiving your free shipment. Simply complete your details below and return the entire page to the address below. *You don't even need a stamp!*

**YES!** Please send me 4 free Medical Romance books and a surprise gift. I understand that unless you hear from me, I will receive 6 superb new titles every month for just £2.40 each, postage and packing free. I am under no obligation to purchase any books and may cancel my subscription at any time. The free books and gift will be mine to keep in any case.

M0ZEA

Ms/Mrs/Miss/Mr ...............................Initials.....................................
                                                                BLOCK CAPITALS PLEASE
Surname ..........................................................................................

Address .........................................................................................

...........................................................................................................

.............................................................Postcode................................

**Send this whole page to:**
**UK: FREEPOST CN81, Croydon, CR9 3WZ**
**EIRE: PO Box 4546, Kilcock, County Kildare (stamp required)**